The Real Ghostbusters

Movie Magic

A novel by Mark Daniel

Carnival

Carnival
An imprint of the Children's Division,
part of the Collins Publishing Group,
8 Grafton Street, London W1X 3LA

Published by Carnival 1988
Reprinted 1988

ISBN 0 00 194301 4

Printed and bound in Great Britain by
William Collins Sons & Co. Ltd, Glasgow

Chapter One

I knew we were in trouble the moment I saw Janine's face.

I mean, Janine thinks of herself as tough, efficient and ultra-cool. She's the sort of secretary that polishes her nails while playing the minute-waltz on the typewriter in thirty seconds flat. Gallantry and deeds of daring – I have noticed – move her not. Panic and terror – I have heard the others observe – have no effect on her. Those gloomy lips neither tremble nor pale; those glasses remain ice clear. If King Kong shoved a paw through her office window, she would lean back in her seat, deliver some supposedly humorous one-line put down such as 'Get a manicure, dog-breath', slap his knuckles and get on with whatever it is she finds to do.

When, therefore, we returned to the fire-station to find her at the top of the staircase, shifting from foot to foot like a sprightly circus elephant, with a colour that looked suspiciously natural in her cheeks, something had to be badly wrong.

We had been chasing up some pretty standard mega-gross composite spooks out in the suburbs, as I recall. I was bruised and tired and all I wanted to do was to sink down into a deep armchair and a deep pizza and reflect upon the Mysteries of the Universe. What I did not want was Janine jumping up and down and clapping like a kid on Christmas Eve squeaking, 'Hey, you guys! Guess who called!'

'Surprise us,' I sighed. I unstrapped my proton-pack and slumped gratefully into my chair.

'Don't start relaxing, bozo,' she grinned, 'we are off on a trip.'

'What is it?' asked Ray, the youngest member of our team, who is inclined to show an immature degree of keenness.

'An hour ago,' Janine wriggled rather repulsively, 'I got this call.'

'Yeah?'

'Yeah. It was a guy.'

'So you've found an admirer. Well, hurrah for short-sightedness.'

'Shut it, birdbrain,' she said with the clipped, respectful precision of the perfect secretary.

'So who was it?' urged Winston.

'You'll never believe me.'

'So why tell us?'

'It was . . .' she paused for the drumroll, '. . . Jacob von Finkelstein!'

'I believe you, Janine, I believe you.' I swung my feet on to the coffee table. 'Has anyone seen my slippers? The ones with the blue bobbles on them. They were here when we left, I'm sure . . .'

'Who,' droned Egon wearily, 'who *is* Jacob von Finkelstein?'

'Oh, come on, Egon, honey. Everyone knows who Jacob von Finkelstein is.'

'Bad luck, Egon,' I yawned, 'you and I are hereby relegated to non-persons.'

'I *think* I've heard of him . . .' mused Winston.

'Dark Moonlight!' cried Janine, exasperated. 'We Met on the Matterhorn! Terror of the Black Lagoon! Love in Lombardy! Skulls of Matebeleland! Blood-Soaked Beast from the Pharoah's Tomb!'

'Stir Well and Season to Taste!' I yawned.

'Yes!' she enthused, then frowned and aimed a kick at my calf. 'No, but you must know. He's a film director! One of the Hollywood legends!'

'I'll buy the tee-shirt,' I sighed.

'So we're going to Hollywood! Tonight! He's making this big movie starring Craig Clyde . . .' she spoke these last words in the same tone as that which actresses use in commercials for packet soups, then closed her eyes and sighed in the approved manner. 'And they're having trouble with ghosts on set, Scottish ghosts I think he said, in an old romantic castle they've rebuilt, and he wants us to go out to Hollywood for a whole month and just think, a whole month in Hollywood with Craig Clyde, and Mr von Finkelstein said I had the most beautiful voice so – let's go!'

She drew breath and gazed with sparkling pride about the room. It was lovely to look at.

'No,' I said.

''Fraid there's too much to do in New York, Janine,' said Winston.

'I've got work to do on Ecto 1,' Ray sighed, (Ecto 1 is our customised ambulance) 'and if they insist on bringing haunted castles to California, I reckon they deserve all they get. Sounds like a publicity stunt to me.'

'Yeah, I'm sorry, Janine,' Egon smiled meekly. Janine mothers Egon. 'But we can't leave our own city unprotected for that long, even in exchange for sunshine and luxury and money. It would be ignoble and unworthy of the high dignity of The Real Ghostbusters. Besides,' he added, frowning, 'who would feed my fungus?'

Slimer too made his opinion felt.

I have not mentioned Slimer until now because – well, because I'd sooner never have to mention Slimer.

Take a large balloon, fill it with slime and give it a slow puncture. Give it two three-fingered hands, two beady little eyes and a huge mouth, and you've got a Slimer.

Slimer is a ghost, which is one good reason to dislike him. His complexion is another. Lurid green looks OK on a lettuce, but not on a floating beanbag. Then there's the fact that he wants to please. I hate people who want to please. It's bad enough to dislike someone without having to feel guilty about it too.

Other people complain about their puppies. 'Bobo left little messages on the carpet,' they say, or 'Fido ate your chicken dinner.' I'll swap Slimer for Bobo or Fido any time. Slimer leaves a trail of ectoplasmic slime on everything he touches, and eats anything that can loosely be described as food. I say he eats it. He inhales it. It just goes down with a slurp of his whiplash green tongue.

Anyhow, Slimer cast his vote with the rest of us. Ghosts, you will discover, are conservatives. They have no great interest in progress. Natural enough, I suppose. That's why they sometimes haunt the same building for centuries. Slimer's like that. He doesn't like to leave the fire-station. He shook his head and looked pathetic and creaked repeatedly like an old rocking chair.

Janine stood with her legs apart and folded her arms. She started on him first. 'I suppose there's no point,' she said casually, 'in telling you that the film company will pay all our expenses, including as much food as we may want?'

Slimer suddenly started to bob up and down. His little eyes widened. That huge curling tongue licked luxuriantly all over his face. He said something very much like 'Wow!' He beamed.

Janine turned to Egon. Her argument to him was straightforward. 'Egon,' she rapped, 'we're going. I've already arranged for your fungus to be looked after, so there.'

Egon blinked at her and gave a goofy grin. 'OK, Janine,' he said.

'I suppose no-one's interested in the fact that Louella Rossini co-stars?' Janine sang.

'I think Janine's got a point,' Ray said, promptly. 'We shouldn't restrict ourselves. Those guys on the West Coast need us as much as anyone else. Everyone should know, they gotta spook, they can rely on the Ghostbusters.'

'You took the words out of my mouth,' Winston nodded eagerly. 'I feel that artists like Louella Rossini, who bring so much joy to this humdrum world, deserve our protection.'

Janine strode over and stood glowering above me. 'So, Bimbo?'

'So?' I glanced up. 'So no. I don't like leaving New York. You know that. I can feel the level of civilization dropping with every mile I go from Times Square. It hurts. Once I saw this TV series called *Civilization*. This guy kept blinking and wandering through cold old joints filled with statues of cold old guys, and saying, "What could be more agreeable?" OK. Fine. Each to his own. That may be his idea of civilization, but it sure as heck ain't mine. First programme in my series called *Civilization* concentrates on the history of the mushroom and anchovy pizza. Second . . .'

'Oh, by the way,' Janine broke in, 'Mr Finkelstein said he was talking six figures minimum.'

'For Pete's sake, Janine,' I stood up. 'Why didn't you say it was an emergency?'

Chapter Two

The metal detectors at the airport played the third movement of Bartok's second String Quartet as we passed through. This, I thought, was a mistake. Something more consoling – a Requiem, perhaps – would, to my mind, have been more suitable, particularly since, a moment later, the customs decided to take a close interest in us. I have always held that Egon has a suspicious face.

They were particularly fascinated by the Proton Guns and the PKE meters, and it took over two hours to satisfy their curiosity. Still, I, like most craftsmen, do not mind explaining the mysteries of my trade to laymen. In fact, I was quite sorry to be dragged away by the others, who do not share my interest in teaching.

The journey to LA was boring, and soon after take-off the others were sprawled and snoring.

Which gives me a chance to explain a thing or two.

My dear old aunt Jessie, God rest her (and I mean that most sincerely) brought me up to be neat and tidy. I'm the sort of guy that straightens pictures and bends down to pick up hundred dollar bills if people leave them lying around. I like things orderly.

And what I say is, if you're dead, you should stay that way. You get up, start monkeying around, scaring honest American citizens out of their so-called wits, it gets me all irritated. It's untidy sort of behaviour.

I mean, most of us live out our three score and ten, get dead then just lie down and keep quiet. That's upbringing, that is. But you'd be surprised at the number of apparently sensible, respectable people that suddenly start itching as soon as they're laid to rest, and take it into their heads to go messing with things that no longer concern them, viz. the living. I hate people who can't stay still.

I've known ex-bank-managers and ex-preachers, ex-dukes, ex-earls and such that just could not lie down and keep quiet. Instead of mouldering like you're meant to moulder, they got up, stretched and thought 'A haunting we will go'.

And boy, were they ever hammy. That's one of the things about spooks. No imagination. No originality. Dead, as it were, from the neck up.

Professor Theophilus Gropius, for example, one of the world's ace physicists. After a lifetime of hard work and regular churchgoing, Gropius strikes out. No sooner is the ink on the obituaries dry than he decides to go in for a little spare-time spooking. Does he come back and give us the latest $e=mc^2$ type info from beyond the grave? Does he heck. He runs up and down the aisles of a supermarket dressed in a sheet and all he can say is 'Wooooooo!' No Nobel Prize for that kind of information.

Add to these reluctant stiffs the usual quota of trolls, troglodytes, ghouls, monsters, blobs, things, succubuses, incubuses, omnibuses and other anti-social elements, and you'll see that we're kept pretty busy. It's tough being a ghostbuster.

'Cos bust 'em is what we do. No question. When you see a big green gluppy thing with red eyes (six), sharp teeth and claws and an unfriendly expression on his face, there is a school of thought that says you should ask him in for coffee, lay him down on the couch and ask when did the trouble start and was it bad potty-training made him that way.

Uh-uh.

When I see a big green gluppy thing with red eyes (six), sharp teeth and claws and an unfriendly expression on his face, I zap him.

Direct, that's me. Sensitive, courageous, all that stuff, but straight down the line when it comes to spooks. It's that decisiveness which makes me the leader of the group. The others don't realize, of course, that I *am* the leader, but that's just because I'm an unassuming, quiet sort of guy. Venkmann's the name. Dr Peter Venkmann.

The trouble with the others is, they're too specialized, too limited. You'll see what I mean if you look at them.

Take Egon. Please? Egon's our egghead, our

walking encyclopaedia. Useful enough in our business since we can hardly lug forty three volumes in luxurious gold-tooled iguana skin around with us. He's the soft-cover portable version.

Trouble with encyclopaedias is, they use the same long-winded, high falutin tone whatever they're describing. Fine when one wants to know about Ziegler's electroprotoectoplasmatrophic theorem, as one does from time to time, but a darned nuisance when it comes to, say, bats. The other day, when in mortal danger, I ducked as a bat flew low over my head and I gasped, as you do, 'What the . . . ?'

Mistake.

'*Pipistrellus pipistrellus*,' twanged Egon, still firing his proton gun at the advancing goblins, 'a flying mammal of the order *chiroptera* or hand-wing, belonging to the family *Vespertilionidae* as distinct from *Rhinolophidae*. The echo-location system of the common bat . . .'

He would still have been gibbering now had a particularly large and intelligent goblin not at that moment pitched him through the window. Every cloud has a silver lining.

Then there's Ray. Sweet guy, practical, but innocent as the day is long. Everything for Ray is all 'Gee whiz! Wow! Amazing!' You or I meet a genuine twelve-foot high troll, we do something constructive, like blow it out of existence or beat a dignified retreat. Ray wants to measure its big toe and compare it to the one recorded by Hans von Strasburg-zu-Essen-und-change-at-Munchen-vür-Mannheim in 1642.

Enthusiasm gives me a sharp pain above the ears. And in the neck.

And last, there's Winston. Winston is all heart. No head of course. All heart. I fear too that he is becoming somewhat hard of hearing. Again and again, when things start getting tricky, I have given the order to withdraw, and again and again Winston has lingered behind, blasting away with a saintly smile on his face. That is the sort of silly mistake that gets people hurt. I must talk to him about it some day.

That then – plus a green glob with the appetite of a vacuum cleaner and a clever-dick star-struck secretary – is the team that I led that night to Los Angeles, California, to contend with a gaggle of imported ghosts and a load of Hollywood film weirdoes. I should have known that we were bound for disaster.

Aunt Jessie (God rest her soul) used to tell me to get a real job.

Great intelligence runs in my family.

Chapter Three

Los Angeles was dismally predictable. There was smog, and somewhere beyond it there was sun. There were lots of gleaming limousines and lots of glamorous people running about.

Ray stayed behind at the airport to drive Ecto 1 up to the studios. The rest of us got into a limo which was really a bus, only they'd sliced off the top layer, thrown out the old seats and put in things like bars and walnut shelves for flowers and telephones and televisions and probably a washing-machine and a cat litter if I'd know where to look. The chaffeur looked like an Oscar statue with clothes and had about as much conversation. His grey uniform cracked rather than creased at the elbows and knees.

'I'll take you to your hotel,' he said dully.

'Uh-uh,' I shook my head. 'The hotel will wait. Let's take a look at the scene of the crime.'

'Those aren't my orders,' the chauffeur droned.

'They are, you know,' Winston assured him with a friendly smile.

'OK, OK,' he sighed. 'So we go see Mr von Finkelstein, but he chews my head off, you tell him it was on your say so, right?'

'You got it,' I assured him, and sat back
enjoy the scenery.

I didn't much. We passed Hollywood. I know
that because there were oversized letters halfway
up the hillside informing me of the fact. I knew
that we were nearing the United Mammoth Movietron Productions set too, because there aren't
many huge turreted white Scottish castles in the
immediate area of Los Angeles. French chateaux,
yes, Greek temples, sure, Thames Bridges,
Roman theatres – but this, I swear, was the only
turreted white Scottish castle that I saw on the
trip.

The car floated to a halt in the midst of canvas
chairs and cameras. We stepped out and surveyed
the scene – all except Egon, who was already busy
with his PKE meter, checking out the level of
Psycho-Kinetic Energy.

Beneath the walls of the castle, a lot of guys in
red tartan skirts were beating a tree against the
front door. No-one seemed to be in. A vaguely
familiar guy with glossy, slicked-back hair was
waving a sword over his head and playing the
cheerleader.

'Craig Clyde!' Janine breathed in my ear.

'Why doesn't he just ring the bell?' I asked.

'Don't be stupid,' she said disdainfully. 'They're
storming the castle. That's a battering ram.'

'Shall I lend him my proton gun?' I suggested.

She sniffed and turned her back on me. Imme-
diately in front of us, cameramen and sound men

17

and continuity girls bustled around doing things with cameras and sounds and continuity. A big, round man sat high above us on a sort of out-of-control dentist's chair on top of a pneumatic lift. He peered through a viewfinder at the guys with the tree.

Suddenly the warlike cries from the castle turned to squeaks and shrieks of disgust. I looked up.

'Hell!' said Winston, 'surely that's . . .'

'Couldn't be anything else,' I said grimly. I unslung my proton gun. 'Time for the Ghostbusters to step in.'

The guys in skirts were running back towards us, their faces twisted in horror, their eyes wide and staring. Their kilts clung to their legs, their hair to their heads. Someone or something on the battlements had defended the castle. But it was not boiling oil which streaked the castle walls and dribbled from the actors' hands. It was thicker and it shone with a strange green light. We knew what it was at once. We should.

Ectoplasmic slime.

'Keep 'em rolling!' shouted the fat man. 'Keep filming! And . . .' as the last of the actors fled past us, 'Cut!'

Winston, Egon and I grouped together and walked forward. 'We'll deal with this,' I reassured everyone. 'Stand back . . .'

'No! No!' the fat man noticed us for the first time. 'Vait, please! Vait!'

We stopped. The pneumatic lift hissed as the chair sank back to ground level. The fat man hopped out and scurried over to us. He had a suede shirt, yellow and black tartan breeches and knee-length boots. His eyes were bulging and pale porcelain blue. He looked crazy as a loon to me.

'You vill be ze Kostbusters, ja?' he whispered.

'Ja.' I grinned. 'Or rather, yeah. I'm Peter Venkmann.'

'Jacob von Finkelstein, vorld-famous film director of cheenius,' he clicked his heels. 'I am klad you could come so kvikly, but I gave instructions zat you shoult be taken to your hotel.'

'Not your driver's fault,' I said. 'It's just we don't like to hang about when it comes to spooks. We, after all, are here to save the world.' I'm always saying things like that. I don't know why.

Finkelstein seemed nervous. Throughout my charming speech he had been glancing over his shoulders and screwing up his face as though in pain. I thought I'd calm him down, so I introduced the others. Janine wriggled a great deal and used a soft, purring sort of voice that I had never heard before.

'Right,' said Winston, stealing my lines as usual. 'Let's get up to that castle. We'll spring-clean your spooks in no time.'

'No, no!' Finkelstein flapped his hand as though burned and again looked over his shoulders. 'Not immeechatly. You vill vant to relax a little, no? Ja!'

19

He tried to steer us back towards the limo, but I shook off his hand. 'We're not in a relaxing kind of business,' I informed him. 'You bring out your dead, we shove 'em in the containment unit, you pay the check, we go back home. Easy.'

'Sh!' Finkelstein was jumping now and his head was spinning. 'Ja, ja,' he stroked his gleaming head with the heel of a hand, 'but I am afrait it is not so simple. I haff to talk to you first. Zis is not sufficiently prifate.'

'Can we see the stars, Mr von Finkelstein?' Janine throbbed in her new soft voice.

'Stars?' Finkelstein frowned and looked skyward, then shook himself and gave a weak grin. 'Ah!' he cried. 'The stars! Ja! Tear, tear Louella and sweet, luffly Craig, you mean, and tarlink, tarlink little Baby Choey, hmm?'

'Baby Joey Allison?' Janine cooed. 'That dear little boy? *He's* in this film?'

'Ja, ja. Baby Choey iss Angus Cameron, nine-year-old heir to ze Laird of Kilmoraig. You vill meet zem all, my frients. You vill meet zem all! But, at ze moment, I fear, Louella and tarlink Baby Choey are in zeir caraffans, a little – intisposed, shall ve say, and tear Craig is vashing off ze special effect you chust saw.'

'That was no special effect,' Egon shook his head. 'That was an ectoplasmic suppuration . . .'

'Sh!' Finkelstein looked as though he was trying to take off. 'Please keep your voice down!' His accent had suddenly vanished. He beckoned and we huddled around him in order to listen to his whispered words of wisdom. 'Listen, guys,' he pleaded, 'please go to your hotel. No-one must know who you are or what you're here for. As far as we're concerned, there are no ghosts, OK?'

'So what are we doing here?' Winston shrugged.

'I'll explain later,' Finkelstein hissed. 'Just settle into your rooms, have a meal, a drink, a swim, anything. I'll join you in a couple of hours, OK?'

'S'pose so,' Winston's lips twitched. 'You're the guy who pays the bills.'

'Great, yeah,' von Finkelstein stepped back and clapped me on the shoulder. 'Ist ferry goot!' he shouted for the benefit of his crew. 'Ferry goot! You,' he stabbed a fat finger at our chauffeur, 'take zese chentlemen to zeir hotel and be kvick about it. I, Jacob von Finkelstein, command it.'

Our own personal Oscar cracked at the waist. 'Sure, Mr von Finkelstein.' He opened the rear door of the limousine and gestured us in like a housemaid sweeping dirt under the carpet. 'Absolutely Mr von Finkelstein.' He slid into the driver's seat. He let out the handbrake. 'Silly jerk,' he muttered under his breath.

Chapter Four

'Hey!' cried Winston, 'It talks, it walks, it says "mama", it's human. Hooray!'

'Come off it, will ya?' the chauffeur spoke into the rear-view mirror. 'You guys don't know what it's like. Anyone I drive might just be the director or the talent scout who's gonna notice me an' say, "Hey, you're just what we're looking for!" I always have to be on best behaviour, always have to look my best. It's like that in this town. It gets tough when you've got guys like Jack Fink playing the great director. I'd like to land one on that guy.'

'Jack Fink?' I grinned.

'Sure,' he shrugged. 'You don't believe all that von Finkelstein stuff, do you? He's Jack Fink from Flatbush.'

'I don't believe a word of it,' snapped Janine. 'He's a great artist. You're just jealous.'

She sulked all the way back to our Beverley Hills hotel.

It was all right as hotels go. I mean, I don't place much store by large blue swimming pools and huge glittering rooms with heart-shaped beds and showers with gold taps and things like that. I'm a tough, simple sort of guy. But if someone insists on giving me all these little luxuries, I'm not so mean as to complain.

Ray was waiting for us by the pool. I wondered for a moment if the flight had affected him, for he seemed to lack his usual youthful energy. He lay with a long cool drink in his hand as we told him what we had seen. Occasionally he said 'hmm', but otherwise did not react. His mind seemed to be wandering. His eyes did not focus on me as I described the quantity of ectoplasmic slime that we had seen; they did not sparkle as Egon related the exceptionally high PKE reading at the castle. They just seemed mistily to follow the girls in bikinis who strolled about the pool.

We left him to sleep it off. I took a shower and tested the heart-shaped bed for a few minutes. I descended to the foyer refreshed and looking really rather dashing.

'Excuse me,' a thin, middle-aged guy in baggy trousers stepped forward and blinked at me through thick glasses, 'are you with the United Mammoth Movietron Productions party?'

'Yep,' I smiled indulgently, 'and I'd be happy to oblige. You got a pen?'

'A pen?'

'Or would you rather I signed in lipstick? No problem. Just hand me the autograph book, son. I haven't got time to waste.'

'I am the manager, sir,' he said dolefully.

'Don't worry about it. No need to be ashamed. We'll pretend it's for your granddaughter.'

'I don't want your autograph, sir.'

'No?' I shook my head. 'May your descendants forgive you.' I muttered, and made to pass him.

He followed me. 'I suppose you're aware,' he said sternly, 'that you are not permitted to have parties in your rooms without prior consultation with the management.'

'Thank you,' I stepped out on to the tiles around the pool and breathed deep of the warm air, 'I am enriched. I have lived all my life without that knowledge. I will pass it on to all my friends.'

'And at least one member of your group has been entertaining a large number of guests in his or her room.'

'I doubt it,' I raised my eyebrows. 'We only arrived an hour ago, and we don't know many people in this area.'

'Nonetheless,' he lisped with irritating precision. 'True, we have been unable to actually find these people . . .'

'So how do you know they're there?'

'It pains me to say this,' he said with the air of a cannibal forgiving the missionary for causing him indigestion, 'but no matter how many people are hidden in cupboards and bathrooms, the room service check will tell its tale. Or are you asking me to believe that five people can eat twenty-seven T-bone steaks and forty-three Meringues Chantilly in the space of an hour?'

Light dawned.

'Yes,' I said, 'I am. You shouldn't have preconceptions, my good man. You Californians may be content with two lentils and a gram of cottage cheese, but we New Yorkers like to eat. Not, of course, to excess. Just enough to keep up our average, unexceptional but essentially phenomenal, strength. Which reminds me. I should think our secretary will be getting a bit peckish by now. Send her up thirty-one half-pounders, medium rare, please. Thank you.'

I don't usually do Slimer favours, but that manager jerk had to be taught respect. Next time, he won't refuse my autograph.

He showed considerably more respect when Finkelstein swaggered into the hotel a short while later. Finkelstein now wore a huge black coat with an astrakhan collar which dwarfed him. One waiter started to tap-dance. Another produced a rather startled-looking rabbit from his sleeve. Another threw off his shirt and tie and flexed his muscles. Finkelstein growled and flapped them away with his fly-whisk.

'Vere are my frients?' he demanded.

'By the pool, Mr von Finkelstein,' the manager bowed.

Finkelstein casually brushed aside the barman who stood on his head in the doorway. He swaggered out and blinked around the pool. Various men at once struck poses. Three or four women jumped into the swimming pool and started, noisily, to drown.

Finkelstein turned to our little group. He

nodded once. 'Find me a room,' he commanded the manager, 'a prifate room vere I can talk viz my frients. Unt send up two bottles of champagne.'

'Certainly, sir,' the manager sang in a sudden, surprising baritone, 'Anything that you say, sir. Your wish is my command!' He finished on a ringing high C. His face was very red.

'Mad,' barked Finkelstein. 'Stark, starink mad. Vere is my room?'

'Yes, sir,' the manager mumbled tearfully. He bowed his head. 'If you will come this way,' he whimpered.

We were shown into a large conference-room. Finkelstein threw off his coat with a sigh and sank into the chair at the head of the table. 'Zis is most emparassing,' he mopped his brow. 'Vere is zis champagne?'

'Janine,' I spoke with natural authority, 'Champagne.'

'Peter,' she sat and crossed her legs, 'Coca Cola.'

One day, I must deal with that girl.

Ray leaped forward and dispensed champagne. Von Finkelstein gulped gratefully. We all settled down around the table.

'Now,' said Finkelstein, 'Vere to start? Zat is ze kvestion.'

'Try Flatbush,' I said.

Chapter Five

Von Finkelstein looked up sharply. He frowned. He planted his fists on the table and puffed himself up like a corpulent cobra. His jowls shook. The pink spots in his cheeks spread until they covered his whole face.

'I'm sorry, Jack,' I said, 'but it's such an effort listening to all that *cherman* stuff. I mean, sure, you have to do that for the troops, but not for us, OK?'

A grin tugged at his lips. A twinkle entered his eyes. He let out the breath in one long sigh and returned to his usual size. 'How do ya know?' he grinned.

'It's our business to know,' I lied. 'We always research our clients.'

'Yeah, well, that makes things a whole lot easier. Now listen. I've asked you guys along because you're the experts. That castle I bought, *Dunmoanin*, it's called – it's a goldmine. We brought it over from the Highlands brick by brick, and no sooner was it built than these spooks started showin' up.'

'Have you seen them?' asked Egon.

'Not seen them, exactly, no,' Finkelstein shook his head, 'but, boy, have I heard 'em and felt 'em.

First thing that happened, before we even had the roof on, the builders walked out or, to be more accurate, ran out. They said they kept hearing these conversations, only there weren't no-one there to be conversating, if you get me. I didn't believe 'em at first, but sure enough, I go up there and I'm all alone in the great hall and I hear all this arguifying going on. I didn't understand it all 'cos it was all in Scotch accents, but the gist of it was, they were discussing what to do with us. They weren't . . .' he blushed and frowned at the memory, 'very complimentary. One of 'em wanted to throw me in the moat, which I didn't fancy much seein' as how I happened to know that we hadn't yet filled the moat. Another of them liked the idea of using me for sword practice. Not friendly. Not friendly at all. So I got out real quick, right?'

'A wise and well-considered move,' I nodded.

'Right. Then at night these spooks start throwing parties and we get complaints from the neighbours about the noise. Some of them said it sounded like they were murdering cats, but our Scotch consultant says that's what they call music. Strange guys, these Scots. Their idea of a party seems to be; lay on some music that sounds like cats being murdered, swear a lot and try to knock one another's heads off.'

'Sounds like home sweet home,' drawled Janine.

'Yeah, well then a coupla days ago we start shooting. First thing that happens, a claymore –

that's what the Scotch call their broadswords –
flies through the air and sticks in the woodwork a
couple of inches from Craig Clyde's expensive
head. Next thing, we're shooting a big banquet
scene. The whole table suddenly tips up and the
spooks are killing themselves laughing as Louella
and Baby Joey dig their way out of a pile of roast
chickens and boars' heads and trifles and such.
Yeah, OK,' he sighed happily, 'I was killing myself
laughing too and so were most of the crew, but
Louella was spitting mad and Baby Joey's mother
says she's gonna sue us for twenty-five million
bucks for the shock to the kid's nervous system. I
could defend the case by pointing out that the kid
hasn't got a nervous system, but that wouldn't be
too good for business. Since then, we've had an
expensive camera – oh, and three cameramen –
thrown from the tower into the moat, and there's
been all sorts of wailing and moaning and mutter-
ing and at least fifty percent of the cast are having
nervous breakdowns, and that's why I called you.'

He sighed deeply, drank deeply and held out
his glass. Ray filled it up.

'So,' said Winston, 'you want us to go in and
bust these ghosts, right?'

'No,' Finkelstein squeaked in alarm. 'I want you
to look after them!'

Professor Theophilus Gropius, deceased, whom
I have already had cause to mention, once
described us as 'four minds with but a single
thought'. He rather unkindly added, 'if that',

which was unnecessary. At the moment when Finkelstein spoke those words, the description (less the last two words) could not have been more appropriate. The Ghostbusters spoke as one. We said, '*What*?'

'I want you to look after them,' Finkelstein repeated simply.

We stared at him. The man was, of course, insane. Do you invite a fox in and tell him to tuck the chickens in at six and please treat the place like his own? Does Herod work for Save the Children? Would you pick Dracula for night-watchman at the Blood Donor Centre? Do leopards promote Clearasil? These and other questions ran through our astonished minds.

Winston was the first to recover his breath. 'Excuse me,' he said, 'but I think you've made some sort of mistake. We are The Ghostbusters. That means we bust ghosts. We don't like ghosts. We certainly do not nanny ghosts.'

I nodded. 'Let's get this straight,' I told Finkelstein. 'You have ghost trouble. It's messing up the shooting of your movie. Why, then, do you not want these hairy highland haunters zapped?'

'Because they're priceless!' Finkelstein stood and started pacing up and down the room. 'Do you know how much I'd have to pay for special effects like they provide? Flying swords! Slime pouring from the battlements! Clyde Craig flying about the room! I mean, that's just a sample of what these spooks can do. I want you to negotiate

30

with them, be nice to them, offer them contracts, get them to work with us.'

'But is this a horror movie?' Egon wanted to know.

'It's whatever they make it, son!' Fink clapped Egon on the shoulder. 'Sure, it started as a romantic little saga about a governess and a Scottish rebel, but we can keep the original storyline and just turn it into a haunted castle. It'll be a sensation!'

'But what about your actors?' I leaned forward, exasperated, 'I mean, you can hardly say to Louella Rossini, "OK, doll, you're co-starring with a load of long-dead Caledonian zombies." She'll be off the set and in the law-courts before you can say Jack Fink.'

'But that's the point!' Finkelstein sat heavily in his chair, emptied the champagne bottle and turned it upside down in the ice-bucket. 'I don't want her or any of the rest of them to know! I've already told them I've got an entirely new sort of special effects, and that I'm gonna surprise 'em so as to get their real reactions. All you have to do is get these ghosts to control themselves a bit.'

'No,' I said, 'I'm sorry. This isn't a job for us. It would take weeks that could be spent busting hundreds of other ghosts. We have a responsibility to mankind, a responsibility which we must self-lessly fulfill, regardless of danger and discomfort. Ours is a cold and lonely destiny, but duty calls and must be answered.'

Finkelstein did not seem to have heard me. 'I propose,' he said, 'to pay each of you twenty-five thousand dollars a week plus expenses.'

Have you ever had that feeling that you've been here before? I felt that as Finkelstein spoke. And suddenly light broke within my brain and I knew with absolute certainty that we were meant to do this job, that this was an essential step on life's rocky highway. Who knows what causes these startling moments of enlightenment? Who knows what deep subconscious stirrings bring wisdom, what divine, angelic or ancestral voice whispers in our ears and makes us suddenly see clearly and with dazzling insight? It is not for us to reason why. Ours is only to accept such revelations with gratitude and to have the courage to admit that, until that moment, we have been blind.

I spoke out Courageously. 'I've been blind,' I said.

Chapter Six

We went up to Dunmoanin castle that very night.
It had looked quite light and airy by daylight but
now you could see that this was a building
designed for battle. The walls were sheer. The
battlements gleamed in the moonlight like bared
teeth. The doors and loopholes were black and
menacing as eye sockets in a skull. I shivered as I
stepped from Ecto 1.

'What have we got on *Dunmoanin*, Ray?'

Ray reached into his deep pockets and pulled
out his database. He stabbed at it three or four
times. 'Dunmoanin Castle,' he said, 'seat of the
Mactavishes, Lairds of Dunmoanin and the Isles
of Addledaig, hereditary chiefs of the warlike clan
Mactavish, as bloodthirsty a bunch of cut-throats
as the wild, heather-clad hills of Sutherland have
nurtured . . .'

'Ray,' I warned quietly, 'it's cold.'

'Right. Yeah. Just building up a bit of
atmosphere.'

'There's quite enough of that already, thank
you.'

'OK. Well, seems these Mactavishes fought just
about every other clan and they didn't fight
straight neither. They had a blood feud with the

Macdonalds down the road. Stole their sheep for centuries. The last three Mactavishes were called Angus, Murray and Iain and they were the maddest and baddest of the lot. They made a treaty to meet the Macdonalds with twenty-four horses in order to make peace. Only trouble was, the Macdonalds rolled up with three guys on each horse. Massacre. Then they kidnapped the beautiful young Morag Macdonald and stuck her up in the tower. All three of them wanted to be her husband so they had a fight in the great hall and all three of them died. She didn't know they were dead, though, so she chucked herself out of the window. It is said that all four of them haunt the castle.'

'Ah, how I miss those little family tiffs,' I sighed. 'Right, guys. We ready?'

All around me I heard the familiar consoling rattle of the proton-guns, the sound of my comrades answering, one by one, 'Ready.'

We trudged up the slight slope towards the moat. We were still fifty yards from the great door when first we became aware of the noise. I took it for the wind, but the breeze did not so much as lift the hair off my brow. It was a low, throbbing moan, like several people blowing gently over empty bottle-tops. With each step that we took it grew louder until, as soon as our feet touched the drawbridge, the night was filled with wild wailings.

We formed closer ranks and pressed on. The high-pitched wails shivered through the night air like shafts of steel, and now there was a deeper

34

sound beneath them – the rough and ragged sound of men laughing. Winston reached out and touched the door.

'Stand back!' he yelped suddenly. 'It's shaking!'

The studded oak of the door rumbled and creaked. The drawbridge beneath our feet vibrated violently. We leaped back and grasped the shuddering railings just as the door flew outwards with a roar. It smashed against the wall and the wind which emerged from inside nearly knocked me off my feet. The laughter was louder now.

'Come on!' Ray yelled above the gale.

We leaned forward into the roaring wind and charged. We were just over the threshold of the great hall when the gale dropped as suddenly as it had started.

We picked ourselves up with dignity, despite the strident laughter which echoed in the vaults of the hall. We looked around.

The floor was of worn flagstones covered with rush-matting. Above the enormous fireplace, three great broadswords were crossed, flanked by three circular leather shields. The chairs around the long refectory table and the staircase which curled above the hall to the gallery, were carved with death's heads and gaping, staring monsters. There were tapestries of battle scenes all the way down the staircase. Otherwise, the only decoration seemed to consist of animal heads. Stags, boars, bears, giant bulls, wolves and jackals all stared at us from the walls in a disgruntled, expressive sort of way.

Suddenly, one of those rough voices stopped laughing for long enough to bellow, 'By wha' righ' de ye venture tae trespass on *Dunmoanin*, the hame of the clan Mactavish?'

'Er, we're here to make you a proposal,' bleated Egon.

'D'ye hear yon impudent pipsqueak?' the invisible ruffian hooted. 'A proposal! Man, there's only one proposal we'll heed, and yon's that ye do battle, as all must do that enter *Dunmoanin* without invitation.'

'No, no. Honestly. No need . . .' Egon said nervously.

'Nae need, d'ye say?' the spook scoffed. 'Nae need? D'ye hear yon wee four-eyed sassenach, lads?'

A lot of invisible people joined in the laughing and jeering.

It was obviously time for the diplomat of the group to step forward. 'Now listen, you shaggy Scotch windbags,' I said reasonably, 'we came here to try to make a deal with you. We'd have knocked on the door if you hadn't tried to knock us out with it instead. It's not your fault that you're ignorant barbarians. No-one's blaming you. Most people would have ended up like you if they'd had to live in some God forsaken little country with nothing but haggis and sheep to talk to . . .'

36

'Er, Peter . . .' Winston spoke out of the corner of his mouth.

'Please don't interrupt, Winston,' I told him. 'So of course we understand why you are at a disadvantage with the likes of us, but . . .'

'Peter!' Ray gasped, and suddenly something made me duck and crouch. Equally suddenly Egon and Winston were squirting very destructive high-energy ions at a point about a foot away from me.

'What on earth . . . ?' I stammered.

'One of those big broadswords,' Egon said calmly, 'just missed your head by about two inches.'

'Oh,' I said, 'thanks.'

'Spectro-visors on,' he ordered.

I straightened and automatically put on the special glasses which Egon had developed for seeing otherwise invisible phantoms. The clay-more was moving away from us now. Within seconds, it was back in its old position above the fireplace. But by then I had seen the man who carried it and who now scurried back up the staircase, a broad grin on his face.

He was large. By large I mean the size of the average tell-your-strength machine that you hit at a fair, only I didn't fancy striking this man's toes with a hammer to see if his face turned pink. He had red hair and a sandy beard and a face as wrinkled as a walnut, calves like bulls' thighs and forearms like calves. He was laughing and holler-ing as he rejoined the other two spooks on the gallery. 'Wa hae!' he cried. 'Those gadgets really hurt! This is more like it!'

I should explain, I suppose, a thing or two about proton-guns. You can't, fairly obviously, kill a ghost. All that you can hope to do is imprison it. Our proton-guns, which can blow physical creatures to smithereens, merely cause discomfort and disorientation to those who have risen – or sunk – to the metaphysical level. We use them, in general, for defence, and in order to manoeuvre our enemies into the area above a ghost-trap. The ghost-trap, as you probably know from your elementary physics, is a sort of portable ecto-vacuum cleaner. We shove the ghost in there, then tip it out into the ecto-containment unit when we get back home. That, at any rate, is the idea.

Anyhow, the usual reaction of ghouls to a fusillade of ions is, as I say, rage, dismay and acute discomfort. This kilted, red-headed giant, however, seemed quite delighted. 'Och, man,' he kept gibbering. 'It feels right grand! We can hae us a real fight with you wee laddies.'

The other two ghosts seemed equally delighted. One of them, an even bigger man with an explosion of black hair which almost completely covered his very red face, grinned broadly. 'D'ye think they can face the might of the clan Mactavish?' he asked.

'Och no,' said the other, a dwarf beside his brothers, but as broad as they were tall. 'They're nought but little dollies with toy guns.'

38

'You want a fight, we'll give you a fight,' Ray's youthful, impetuous voice echoed in the high ceiling. I wished it hadn't.

'Yeah,' Winston stood, legs wide apart, hips thrust forward, an agressive scowl on his face. 'We are The Real Ghostbusters.'

Some twenty, large kilted warriors stepped on to the gallery behind the three leaders, broadswords drawn and glittering. 'But that's not what we're here for, of course,' I said hastily. Another twenty or so emerged from the doors and gazed down on us. 'Last thing we want,' I said amiably. Twenty more shuffled into place, all large, all hairy. 'Our aim, as I've already said, is to make a deal with you, a deal which will be mutually beneficial . . .'

At least a hundred members of the clan Mactavish stared expressionlessly down at us. 'I think,' I said quietly, 'that we're in serious trouble here.'

Chapter Seven

'Reet, lads,' the black-bearded monster growled, though I could not see his mouth move. 'Why dinna a few of ye gang doon and show yon trespassers what it means tae step o'er the threshold of *Dunmoanin* without an invitation.'

We learned something very interesting about the history of the English language then. If ever you happen to find yourself in early eighteenth century Scotland, do not suggest a brisk hill-walk of 'a few' miles or going down to the pub for 'a few' drinks or having your mother-in-law to stay for 'a few' days. 'A few' you will be intrigued to know, meant 'about thirty, plus two pony-sized, furry dogs.'

They came down the stairs in an orderly enough fashion. They formed up opposite us in absolute silence. Then they charged, and all semblance of good manners fled. They shrieked, they roared, they swung their swords above their heads like helicopters, and somewhere in the background, just to add to the confusion, someone started squeezing and blowing some bagpipes.

We opened fire.

The first blast of ions made them stop and shake their heads a bit. The dogs yelped and scurried back up the stairs with their tails between their legs. The warriors came on.

'Outflank 'em!' Egon ordered. 'Push them over here!'

We wheeled to the left as we fired, driving the screaming warriors round towards the fireplace. We were keeping them at bay about ten feet away from us, but they did not retreat. These guys had hard heads and, just like their redheaded leader, actually seemed to enjoy the battle.

Egon stood over the ghost-trap. He lowered his gun, took two steps back and started behaving in a very un-Egonish way. 'Yah!' he yelled at the nearest Scotsman. 'Great shaggy Scotch maniac! Think you're tough do you? Huh! You couldn't cut the head off a daisy! No wonder you wear skirts . . . !'

The warrior nearest to him shrieked, raised his sword high above his head and swung it like a headsman's axe straight down at Egon's head. Egon smiled happily. Suddenly the ghost's feet were sucked away from him and, with a gasp and a gurgle, he vanished into the ghost trap. The sword clattered harmlessly to the floor.

'Interesting, really,' Egon went on, 'obviously the Scots are as bad at fighting as they are at soccer . . .'

This brought six more screaming spooks flying at him with murder on their minds. They too were gratefully gulped down by the ever-greedy ghost-trap.

41

And so it went on. We pinned them down with proton fire, Egon insulted them and they all charged with joyous fury to their doom. As the last of them vanished like water down the plug, the bagpipes stopped playing. We looked up at the crowd on the gallery. A 'few' more of these loonies were already starting to descend the staircase to take their kinsmen's places.

'Hold!' the big man with the black beard shouted. The whole room shook, 'I'll lose no more brave men of the clan Mactavish in such folly. Yon's a canny wee contraption ye've got,' he nodded to me. 'Would ye teach us how it works?'

'Why?' I demanded.

'Because it would be useful against the vile Macdonald!' he roared. 'I'd like to see them all gulped up by that nice wee machine.'

'But the Macdonalds are in Scotland,' I explained. 'You are now in the United States of America.'

'I know it,' the ghost said dolefully, and from somewhere in the mass of black hair, two drops of water emerged and dripped glistening on to his coat-sleeve. 'Far, far from our beloved hame . . .'

'Far, far from the silver salmon, the mighty roaring rivers . . .' sobbed the one built like a barrel.

'. . . the barking of the seals . . .'

'. . . the haggis and the whisky . . .'

At this, the whole gathering burst into tears.

We stood feeling rather embarrassed as they sobbed and howled and borrowed handkerchiefs.

'Yes, yes,' I said impatiently, 'but what about the Macdonalds?'

The red-bearded chief gulped and sniffed. 'The black-hearted Macdonalds came with us,' he sighed. 'We are the brothers Mactavish. This,' he indicated the black muppet on the right, 'is Angus, Laird of Dunmoanin and Addledaig. I am Murray of the Red Beard and the Red Hand. This,' he turned to his left, 'is Iain the Bullslayer. We killed hundreds of Macdonalds until, by a slight accident, we too became as now you see us. There is a closed season for stags, a closed season for salmon, but never a closed season for Macdonalds. See one, scent one, pursue it and chop its silly head off.'

'Sounds like a sophisticated sort of sport,' I nodded reasonably.

'But for three centuries, those Macdonalds have continued to storm this castle. Every night at midnight they come seeking to recover my rightful wife, Morag . . .'

'My wife,' said Angus.

'Mine,' said Iain.

'Mine!'

'Mine!'

'Mine!'

'I am the laird!'

'I am the champion!'

'I am her favourite!'

'Wilt prove thy claim on thy sword?'

'I'll spit thee like a sucking pig!'

'Vain effort, since I shall cleave whoever remains from his crown to his toes!'

'Draw!'

'On guard!'

'Have at thee!'

'Gentlemen, gentlemen!' I called. 'Much as we would like to see a little skilful swordplay, time is short. Please settle your differences in our absence. Carry on about the Macdonalds.'

Angus spat and sheathed his sword with a clang. 'The Macdonalds,' he said, 'heard that the castle was to be moved to this barbarian land. We should have known that something was wrong when, the night before the move, they did not attack. They were tunnelling, the treacherous swine, and when the castle was rebuilt, they revealed themselves. They had taken possession of the East Tower, and noo, day and night, they do everything in their power to vex us.'

'They couldn't bear to see you go,' I smiled. 'How sweet.'

'You jest?' Iain the Bullslayer growled.

'No, no. Absolutely not. OK, so supposing we were to get rid of the Macdonalds for you, would you help us?'

There was a lot of mumbling at that. At length, Angus leaned over the gallery. 'We'll need more,' he said.

'What more?' Winston shrugged. 'Money can't help you.'

'Not money, lad,' Murray snapped, 'we'll need whisky.'

'How much?' Ray took out his notebook.

'After three hundred years without a dram,' Iain said grimly, 'that's a silly question. I'd say twelve bottles for each man.'

'*Twelve* bottles? A *week*?'

'Twelve bottles a *day*,' Angus said calmly. His army murmured approval. 'And venison,' he said.

'And roast pig!' said someone else.

'Whole oxen!'

'Peacock!'

'Whoah, whoah!' Egon raised a hand. 'We agree to rid you of the Macdonalds and to supply one bottle of whisky per man together with one whole roast ox or stag per day in exchange for your assistance, and that is our last offer.'

There was some more mumbling, then Angus returned to the gallery rail. 'Have ye got Scottish blood?' he asked Egon.

'I don't think so,' Egon said politely.

'Well, ye drive a hard bargain. But ye've got a deal. Now what would ye have us do?'

Chapter Eight

Finkelstein chortled cheerily as we arrived on the set the following morning. He had been delighted by the success of our negotiations. 'Louella!' he called, 'comm and meet my new special effects experts. Zey are machicians, you will see. You vill not so much as notice a mirror or a string. Zey vill constantly surprise you, not so?'

'So,' I assured him.

Louella Rossini glided over in a succession of long, sinuous, serpentine curves. She wore a white shirt and pink satin trousers. She had long dark curly hair and a full painted mouth. Everything about her was full, in fact, except her head. I'm not very big on film stars, but even I had seen pictures and posters of Louella Rossini. She had been married, I think, about six times, and each time the alimony was counted in telephone numbers. Still, she looked OK, so I adopted a casual pose and held out a hand in greeting. She hit me. Hard.

'That,' she said, 'is for the trick with the table. I've never been so scared in my life and I've been washing chicken fat out of my hair for the last three days.'

'Why me?' I blinked, hurt.

''Cos you're standing up front,' she said simply.

She shook hands with the others. Ray and Winston took her hand eagerly and gazed rapturously at their palms as she moved on. Egon, however, appeared not to notice her presence. He was busy adjusting the range-finder on his ghost-detector when she thrust her hand out beneath his eyes. 'Hello,' she said softly.

Egon looked up. He blinked three times, turned his eyes down to his feet then up to the sky, went bright pink and said, 'Um, hello.'

She kept hold of his hand. 'Hello,' she purred, 'I'm Louella Rossini.'

'Yes,' Egon said absently, 'I have – er – long admired your cinematographic work, Miss Rossini, finding it at once elevating and entertaining. Your, um, portrayal of Margaretha Geertruida Zelle, familiarly known as Mata Hari, eighteen seventy-six to nineteen seventeen, was, if I may say so, sensitive and, er, sensuous in the extreme . . .'

'Yeah?' squeaked Louella Rossini. 'Hey, you're cute!'

'Er, thank you,' Egon studied his feet again and blushed still deeper. 'The word "cute", as you are doubtless aware, is an abbreviation of "acute" which derives in turn from the Latin "*acus*", a needle.'

'You don't say,' she stroked his forearm and her eyes glistened. 'And what's this cute little machine you've got there?'

47

'This? Oh, this is to detect . . .'

'It's a special projector which creates illusions,' Winston broke in sharply.

'Who asked you?' Louella snapped.

'Und zis here is Craig Clyde,' Finkelstein said at my shoulder.

I turned. Craig Clyde, hero of a hundred adventures, suave, witty man of the world, tough, hard-hitting cowboy, gallant soldier, daring villain, ruthless crimebuster, stood before me. And beneath me. He was about four foot two in platform shoes.

'Hi!' I said, and instantly wished that I'd thought of another word.

'Put it there,' he swaggered. He turned to Finkelstein. 'I hope, Mr Finkelstein, that you have dismissed that make-up girl and replaced her with someone who knows her business. My cheeks have been crying out for moisture all night. I very nearly did not turn up today.'

'Ja, ja!' Finkelstein soothed. 'Do not vorry, Craigie baby. All vill be vell. You look vonderful today.'

'Yes, well, I suppose I do,' Craig Clyde said modestly.

While the actors went through costume and make-up, we briefed the ghouls of *Dunmoanin* on their roles for the day.

The adapted plot of the film went something like this. Louella, an innocent young girl, arrives at *Dunmoanin* to work as little Alistair Cameron's governess. The laird, stern, brooding widower Craig Clyde, spends a lot of time on mysterious missions, leaving Louella and Baby Joey alone together in the castle. In the original script, they spent a lot of time talking about life without love and why the Laird is so stern and brooding and whether or not he is a traitor to Scotland. The consensus is that he is.

Then a redcoat colonel, played by Sir Quentin Vane, an old English actor, turns up and commandeers the castle and starts forcing his attentions on Louella. Clyde returns, fights off the redcoats, kills the colonel, proves to be the world's greatest spy, working for Bonnie Prince Charlie, hugs Baby Joey and declares his undying love for Louella. All three walk off into the sunset.

Louella says, 'I love you.' Clyde says, 'I love you.' Baby Joey says, 'I love you both.' They gaze back through the gloaming at Dunmoanin, and Clyde says something like, 'and as long as love reigns in Dunmoanin and in the glens and mountains of our beloved land, Scotland will never die.'

Music. Titles. Not a dry eye or an empty sickbag in the house.

Anyhow, now that we had an extra cast of thousands with supernatural powers, it had been decided that, whilst the laird was away, the ghosts would play, frightening the life out of Louella and Baby Joey.

'Talk to these spooks of yours,' Finkelstein said.

49

'See if they have any good ideas. Anything so long as we don't end up with a law suit.'

'Why don't we chop the heads off a few of yon actor chappies?' asked Angus. 'There's nowt like a good decapitation for pleasing the crowds.'

'No,' I sighed, 'I don't think so. Actors are expensive.'

'Can't see why, I must say. I wouldna employ one o' them to mind the pigs. Bodies like prawns and voices like nursery-maids.'

'All the same, we can't have actors' heads chopped off all over the place.'

'Well, the servants, then. It's no' exactly sport-ing, but . . .'

'No!' I struck my brow. 'No, no, no! We need something involving a little less blood.'

'Och,' Iain sighed, 'It's no fun wi'oot a few cuts and bruises.'

'I know,' said Murray. 'Supposing this lassie and the young lad are sitting in the classroom doing their lessons . . .'

'Yes?'

'And suddenly, everything starts to go mad. Start with the doors bangin' and squeakin'. Then the pictures fall fro' the walls. Then the table starts to shift and the books fly up in the air and they scream and try to get to the door, only, as you watch, the door changes to solid oak panelling and the panelling on another wall turns into a door. So they rush for that, and the same thing happens. Then the floor starts risin' and fallin' like the sea,

50

and the spears fly across the room, narrowly missin' the wee bairn . . .'

'Not too narrowly.'

'Nae. A miss is a good as a mile. And then there's the sound of weepin' and wailin' comin' from nowhere . . .'

'You're good at that,' I nodded.

'Och,' he blushed, 'it's just one of the wee things we Mactavishes pride oursel's on. We've had practice, of course.'

'Of course.'

'And then, if you wanted,' he said, warming to his task like a natural film director, 'the walls could start moving slowly inward, crushing the table and the chairs, leavin' them with a just a few inches to move in . . .'

'Yes,' I said, 'and then?'

'Aye,' Murray nodded gravely, 'we've got a problem there.'

'No problem!' roared Angus with glee. 'Then the great war axe of the Mactavishes appears, wielded by an invisible hand, and . . .'

'Chops their heads off?' supplied the Ghostbusters as one.

'Aye!'

'No.'

'World's gone soft, Iain,' Angus said over his shoulder.

'Aye, aye,' Iain muttered.

'No, but wait,' said Ray, 'at that moment, Louella tells baby Joey to fall on his knees and pray, and they both pray, and suddenly everything goes back to normal again.'

'What for?' Angus demanded.

'So as you can torment them again tomorrow,' I explained.

'Aye, aye,' he smiled happily. 'That makes sense.'

'OK,' I stood, 'I'll put it to Mr Finkelstein and see what he has to say. But, listen, guys. You must get it into your heads – no-one is to be hurt, OK?'

'And tonight you get rid of the Macdonalds?' Iain grinned. 'Forever?'

'Forever.'

'And the whisky?' demanded Angus. 'We could do wi' a dram afore a hard day's work . . .'

'Tonight,' I said firmly, 'you can have a party. Today, I want clear heads.'

There was grumbled assent from the spooks around the table.

Finkelstein loved the idea, and it was up to us to explain it to Louella and Baby Joey who, we were told, were in their caravans.

Chapter Nine

We tackled Louella first. She was now dressed in a long white dress with a tartan sash across her. Her hair was piled high on her head. A very humble looking man attended to her nails, while a very ugly secretary in the corner of the caravan sat with pen poised to take down love letters, proposals of marriage, demands for extra alimony or whatever other romantic thoughts came into Louella's lovely head.

'Hi,' I said.

'Oh, you again,' she drawled. 'Yes?'

'Er, we're here to brief you on the special effects for this morning's scene.'

'Shurrup,' said Louella. 'My Egon can tell me, can't you, Egon, baby?'

Egon blushed and studied the caravan ceiling and looked for all the world as though some powerful emotion was affecting him. Ridiculous idea, of course, but a good imitation. He stepped forward. 'Well, Miss Rossini,' he told the floor, 'it has been resolved in consultation with the director and – and others – that whilst you, as governess, are instructing young master Allison, a series of, um, apparently supernatural events will take place, um. And, er, you with your consummate skill in simulating the human emotions, will react, of course, with naturalistic terror. But I can guarantee to you that, er, whatever happens, you will in no way be injured.'

'That's good enough for me, Egon, honey,' she smiled up at him.

Egon sort of shuddered. 'And, when things are at their worst, all you have to do is speak a heartfelt prayer to the Lord, and the metaphysical manifestations will at once cease.'

'Great,' Louella sniffed, 'I pray good. Now, why don't you guys run along'n leave Egon and me alone, hey? You don't know how difficult it is, Egon, honey, having no-one of one's own intellectual capacity on set to talk to. It's such a relief to find a fellow genius . . .'

Ray, Winston and I made ourselves scarce, and did not laugh until we were four steps away from the caravan door.

Next, 'Baby' Joey.

I hammered on the caravan door. 'Go away!' shrieked someone within.

'Er, we want to speak to Joey Allison,' I spoke loudly.

'Who are you?'

'Special effects,' I replied, 'with important information about today's scenes. Mr Finkelstein sent us.'

The door latch clicked. A haggard middle-aged woman with dyed red hair opened the door a crack and peered out. She appraised us as though we were something upleasant on her shoe, then sniffed loudly. 'OK,' she stood back, 'you get two minutes.'

We were ushered into the presence of 'Baby' Joey Allison. He lay on the bed, his pale blonde hair a gleaming halo, his chubby pink and white face serene in apparent sleep.

'I'm Mrs Allison,' said the woman behind us, 'Joey, as you see, is composing himself.'

I cleared my throat. 'Yes,' I said in my best manly tones, 'sorry to disturb you, Joey, but we just wanted a word or two about the effects in this morning's scene.'

The long thick eyelashes arose hesitantly, 'They won't be fwightening, will they?' he said in a small voice.

'Not really, Joey, no,' I sat on the corner of the bed, 'because you'll know that they're just conjuring tricks. You'll know that they can't hurt you. You just have to pretend to be frightened, that's all.'

'Mister,' droned Mrs Allison, 'how many pictures you been in?'

'Um – well, as an actor, very few,' I smiled, 'in fact, not to put too fine a point on it, none.'

'Yeah, well this is Joey's forty-third starring role, so cut the drama coach stuff, will you?'

'Don't be nathty to the nithe man, mummy, pleathe,' murmured Joey. 'He can't help it.'

I considered this. Just what could I not help? Should I thank the little angel or wring his scrawny

55

neck? I did neither in the end, because Winston squatted down by the bed and did his paternal bit. 'No, you mustn't be afraid, Joey,' he urged, ''cos we're gonna be controlling everything and there's nothin' to worry about and you're gonna be a real brave kid, aren't you?'

Joey's angelic eyes turned slowly to Winston and for a moment I thought that I saw a flicker of some less than charitable thought in their liquid depths. 'I twy to be bwave,' he said, 'but it'th difficult.'

'You'll be OK, kid,' Winston grinned. 'I'll never be far behind you.' He slapped his thigh and stood. 'And now, with your permission, Mrs Allison, we'll leave this darlin' little boy to meditate in peace. Come along, Peter, Ray. Leave Joey alone, if you please,' and he ushered us out of the door.

The classroom scene, as directed and conceived by Jacob von Finkelstein and Murray Mactavish (RIP) went like a dream. A bad dream, but a dream nonetheless.

We stood behind the cameras and, like orchestral conductors, nodded to each of the ghosts to tell them when to do their bits. I nodded to the door-bangers. They banged the doors. Egon gave the cue to the picture-droppers. They dropped the pictures.

Then the real fun started. Angus and Iain, invisible to the rest of the crew, stood on either side of the table, a few inches from Louella and Joey. They picked up the table and rocked it. Louella looked suitably mystified and scared. Joey gazed on in wide-eyed wonder. Iain plucked the book from Louella's hands and carried it slowly out of shot. Louella yelped, her face drained of colour. She stood. Angus, with a wicked grin on his face, took the opportunity to lean across and pinch her. She yelped again, this time louder, and knocked over the chair. She clasped Joey to her.

'Save me!' cried Joey, and sobbed affectingly.

Then came the spears. Louella heard them moving, saw them lifted and, as they were hurled, shrieked and rushed for the door. The door turned to panelling.

A spear slammed into it just to the right of her head. Another just to the left. Now she was really frightened. She let out a piercing scream and turned towards the camera, her face twisted by terror.

As for little Joey, he broke free of her grasp pointed at Finkelstein and yelled, 'I'll sue you for every ?*£)¼ cent you @!!(/* got, you qwertyuiop asdfgh!' or words to that effect. He was not very pretty now. His face was puckered and wrinkled like a burst balloon.

Finkelstein was ready for this. 'Cut!' he shouted, then turned to Joey. 'Vot is zis amateur display, Allison?' he demanded. 'You are an actor or not? Never haff I seen such pathetic behaviour! Look at Louella! She, now, is an actress! Ja, she pretends to be frightened, of course, but she is a star! She only pretends!'

We all looked at Louella. She sat slumped on the floor, eyes wide and staring, but at Finkelstein's words, she gave a weak smile, nodded and made a silvery little 'ha ha ha' noise.

'But you – ' Finkelstein pointed, 'you scream and yell abuse like a hysterical rabbit because of some special effects? Ha! I do not direct you. I renounce you. Your moofie career is finished, kaput!'

'But . . .' Joey stammered, and suddenly he resumed his sweetness, 'I wath naturally frightened, Mithter Finkelstein. I . . . I . . .' his eyes filled with tears.

'Nein, nein! Do not start blubbering. It vill do you no good! You are finished, I tell you!' Finkelstein turned and gave me a broad wink, then returned to the attack. 'Did I not tell you zere vere new speical effects men viz a new sort of special effects? Did I not tell you?'

'Yes . . .' Joey sobbed.

'*Do not cry!*' Finkelstein bellowed. 'No-one cries on my set unless I tell him to, is zat understood?'

Joey gulped. 'Yes.'

'You sink zese are real ghosts or somesing? Gentlemen,' he turned to us, 'please to show us vot you can do.'

'OK,' I stood, 'let's have everything back in its place.'

Egon and Ray fiddled with the PKE meter for the sake of the effect. I nodded to the Mactavishes. The spear-throwers wrenched out the spears and replaced them in the corner. The pictures were rehung. Iain picked up the book from the floor and gently replaced it on the table. The table was straightened.

Joey and Louella watched, terrified. Angus moved behind Joey and his bushy eyebrows arose, questioning. I nodded. Angus placed his hands beneath Joey's elbows and lifted. Joey squeaked, remembered himself and susbstituted a fixed grin for his initial grimace of horror. Angus raised him very high – and Angus's high was about nine feet – and lowered the stiff trembling little body into the chair in which he had sat at the outset.

'Hey!' Louella had recovered a little of her colour, 'that looks fun! Can I have a go?'

I nodded to Angus. There was no need. Already he had swung her up into his arms. The cameramen gasped as, lying cradled in invisible arms, Louella floated back to the table. Iain set the chair upright. Angus regretfully deposited her in it. Just as she sat, however, she started forward with a high-pitched yelp. Angus grinned happily. Louella giggled. 'Egon, honey,' she said, 'you're a naughty, naughty boy!' She wagged her finger at him. Egon blushed.

'Pleathe, Mithter Finkelthtein,' Joey said in his tiniest, shakiest voice. 'I'm thowwy. I didn't mean it. I won't do it again, honetht.'

'Ferry vell,' Finkelstein conceded. 'You have von last chance. Now, ve vill start all ofer again from ze beginning. All right? Positions. Camera; and – action!'

Chapter Ten

'Wonderful, wonderful!' Finkelstein, now once more Fink of Flatbush, crowed that evening. 'The shots are wonderful, the effects are wonderful and that disgusting little Joey – oh, boy, I've been longing for an opportunity like that for ages.' He rubbed his hands vigorously together.

'You mean he isn't a sweet little kid?' Ray sounded astonished. 'I mean, fear takes people in some funny ways, you know.'

'Sweet? Sure he's sweet, when there's money in it for him. Little? Oh, yeah, he's little, which is why he's still playing eight-year-old brats at the age of fourteen. Kid? Kid he ain't. Inside, he's a mean old man of about one hundred and forty-six and his mother of sent Methuselah to an early grave.'

'Life,' sighed Ray, 'is full of disillusion.'

'You get used to it, son,' Finkelstein patted his shoulder. 'Now, what tricks can we think up for tomorrow?'

That night, we zapped the Macdonalds. Angus, Murray and Iain accompanied us to the East tower and cheered as each of the forty-three clan members were driven into the ghost-trap. It was almost depressingly easy, for they responded to the presence of the Mactavishes with the same savage joy as that with which some of their bitterest enemies had charged at Egon last night.

'Thus,' pronounced Angus, 'perish all who dare affront the Mactavishes of Dunmoanin.'

'You ever thought of working as a Hollywood scriptwriter?' asked Winston.

And that's when the only complication of the evening occured. A beautiful girl with long red hair floated, weeping through the door. From the tartan of her sash, I knew that she too was a Macdonald.

'Cowards!' she sobbed. 'Craven cowards! What devilry have you employed? What dark arts do these strangers do? Where are my kinsmen? What have you done with them?' She turned her tear-stained face to us and there was hatred in her eyes.

'You have no kin, Morag,' Angus announced flatly. 'They are gone forever. Noo thou must cleave unto thy husband, the laird of Dunmoanin' and the Isles of Addledaig.'

'Never!' she tore her arm from his grasp. 'I'd sooner . . .' and then she remembered that she could not die and she fell to her knees. She covered her face with her hands and sobs shook her shoulders.

'Nay, Angus,' Murray stepped forward and clasped Morag's arm, 'thy words were ay brutish and thy manners rough. Dinna fret, Morag.

Thoult have family and friends enough when thou'rt wed to me.'

She shuddered, wailed like a dog and flung herself forward with a howl.

'Lay off thy hand, Murray,' Iain growled. 'I'll take care of my ain bride, an I'll thank thee.'

'Er, excuse me, Egon,' said Ray. We all turned. He was crouching in the corner packing up the ghost-trap. Now he stood and walked casually across the room, dragging the trap along the floor behind him. 'We seem to have a malfunction in this machine,' he said casually. He reached the centre of the room and gazed down the nozzle of the trap. 'I can't think what's wrong,' he shrugged, and, with a gesture of exasperation, he turned it downward.

'No!' cried Angus, Murray and Iain in unison, but before they could move, Morag Macdonald, with a grateful sigh, floated up like vapour into the trap to join her family forever.

'Sorry,' said Ray simply. 'It is working after all.'

'You did that a-purpose,' Angus barked.

'You killed my wife!' Iain's sword rasped and rang.

'No,' Egon stood, his proton-gun at his hip, 'you killed her. All of you. Nearly three hundred years ago, she took her own life rather than take one of you for a husband, and still you keep arguing that she's yours or yours or yours. Well, she's nobody's. She never has been, because you never gave her the chance to choose. I'm sick and

63

tired of listening to your self-centred ranting. She's haunted this castle for all these years because she was not with her own. Now she's back with them. She can rest. Let her be.'

There was a lot of silence after that. There are many sorts of silence, just like there are many sorts of black. There is the silence of open country, the silence of a cathedral, the silence of a long abandoned house, the silence of an empty theatre, the silence of embarrassment, the silence of lovers and many more. This was the silence of confrontation, the sort that one person or group of people throws at another like a weapon. The Mactavishes stared at us. We stared back.

Ray was the first to break it. He sighed. 'Yeah, well, like I said, I'm sorry. Anyone can make a mistake.'

'And furthermore,' I said, 'we've got fifty-two bottles of whisky and a whole ox waiting for you back in the great hall.'

'Aye,' muttered Angus, 'there's that.'

'Could have been a mistake,' said Murray.

'Could have been,' Iain sheathed his sword.

But their admission was grudging. Our treaty, just twenty-four hours old, was over, I think, from that moment on.

The following morning the Mactavishes were grumpy and morose. Angus clutched his hairy head and looked like a broken mop. Murray of the Red Beard and the Red Hand could claim a new title relating to his eyes, which were now as red as both, and Iain the Bullslayer eyed us blearily as though trying to decide whether we were, or were not, bulls. They were a touch short on creativity.

'Why should we play party tricks for the likes of you?' Angus groaned.

''Cos we've got a deal,' I smiled.

'Aye, but ye canna make us keep it. The Macdonalds are gone, aren't they? Ye canna bring them back.'

'True,' I said amiably, 'but what about your food and whisky?'

'Dinna mention that word!' Murray roared. Angus gave a deep, heartfelt moan. Iain covered his ears and turned faintly green. 'We never want to see whisky again,' said Murray, subsiding.

'Aye, I'll never touch another drop,' groaned Angus.

'It's the devil's draught,' throbbed Iain solemnly. 'Get thee behind me, Satan!'

'Oh, dear,' I said, and glanced apprehensively at the others. We had not anticipated hobgoblin hangover. 'Well, what about the food?'

Murray shook his head slowly. 'I don't know what it is,' he said sorrowfully, 'but roast venison is no' what it used to be. Perhaps it's that it's no' Scots venison.'

'Aye,' nodded Angus, 'perhaps. Ye wait three hundred years for something, ye dream about it every night, ye're bound to be disappointed when it comes.'

'The very thought of meat,' said Iain, 'makes me sick.'

'Well, of course,' I said cheerily, 'there is the little detail that we will totally destroy you if you don't work for us.'

'Ye'll *what*?' Angus leaped to his feet, rocked slowly for a second or two, then sank back into his chair with a groan.

'We'll zap you, brother,' drawled Winston. 'We'll wipe you out, obliterate you from the face of the earth, annihilate you, efface you, spifflicate, devastate and atomize you.'

'Nicely put, Winston.'

'Thank you, Peter.'

'And, as you are no doubt aware,' I continued, 'in your present state, we could so with the greatest of ease. Your men, I'll warrant, are still fast asleep?'

'The Mactavishes never sleep,' Murray hit the table, 'but yes.'

'Right, then, here's what we're gonna do today . . .'

Chapter Eleven

Janine, who had been touring the stars' homes the previous day, was waiting for us when we emerged from the castle.

'So,' she said, 'spooks co-operating?'

'They have to,' said Ray, 'but they're not happy about it.'

'They've all got heads like toasted marshmallows and mouths full of moths,' said Winston.

'It'll pass, though,' I said confidently. 'By midday, they'll be thinking about their feast tonight and they'll be desperate to please us again.'

'I'm not so sure,' Ray spoke quietly. 'I don't trust 'em.'

'I wouldn't worry. We'll get a month's work out of them and then we'll let 'em have it,' I assured him.

Janine laid a hand on Egon's arm. 'What do you think?' she asked.

'Er,' said Egon vaguely. 'Yes. I think I'd better go and have a quick word with Louella. She needs comforting and reassurance, you know.'

'Don't we all?' Janine snapped at his back as he scampered over to Louella's caravan. 'What's got into that guy?'

We all shrugged in turn. None of us had the slightest idea what was eating him. Whatever it was, it wasn't natural. Egon just didn't do the sort of stupid irrational things that we did, like falling in love.

Suddenly, we ceased to worry about such trivia. We were under fire.

'Hell!' I shouted. Instinctively I dropped and rolled. I clutched my temple. There was no blood, but something had hit me hard and shaken my brains. Above me, the others too shouted and ran for cover. None of us was armed. I started to crawl towards the nearest caravan. Another missile hit me. I clambered to my feet and ran.

Janine was already lying flat beneath the caravan which I chose. I dived in. The coldness and wetness of the ground was soon apparent.

She touched a large red bruise on her forehead and winced. 'It's coming from over there,' she hissed. She nodded towards a caravan opposite.

'Oh, is it?' I said grimly. 'Well, Janine, you are about to meet dear, sweet little "Baby" Joey Allison. You may be the last person on earth to meet dear, sweet little "Baby" Joey Allison. That'll be something to put in your diary. You see, I am now going to kill dear, sweet little "Baby" Joey Allison.'

'OK, guys!' I called. 'Let's take 'em!'

I pulled myself out from under the caravan. I stood. Ray and Winston also emerged. Their boiler suits were stained, their faces coated with grime. Janine followed me out into the middle of the street. I bent and picked up one of the 'bullets'.

It was a pebble. Not just any old pebble, mind you, not your average, run of the mill sort of pebble which abounds on the proverbial beach. This pebble had been selected with care and with malice aforethought. It was a sliver of grey flint with more sharp edges than a cutter could put on a diamond of that size. A stone-age arms-dealer would have swapped two size-ten, Paris-designed mammoth skins for a pebble like that.

The Real Ghostbusters are not attacked with impunity. We strode up to 'Baby' Joey's caravan.

This time, we did not bother to knock. I just threw open the door and we marched in. Joey was once more lying on the bed, looking like an angel. His mother squeaked as we entered. 'What are you doing?' she shrilled. 'This is a star's caravan! It's private property! I'll sue you for everything you've got! Psychological damage, invasion of privacy, breaking and entering, menacing behaviour . . .'

'You forgot assault,' I said.

'You haven't . . .' she stopped and stared. '. . . You wouldn't?'

She reached with a fumbling hand into the drawer behind her. I stood back, expecting a gun, but she was only fetching out her pocket calculator. 'Hold on,' she said, 'what are you going to do to him?'

'Tan his precious hide,' said Janine.

'Nothing else?' Mrs Allison sounded disappointed. 'A little bruising on the face perhaps? I can get five hundred thousand per bruise. Clip him round the ear. He can be partially deafened. That'll be a cool five million . . .' she stabbed frantically at the calculator, 'plus I'll make sure he has nightmares and can't sleep for a few months and that'll affect his work – say five million more – that'll be . . .'

'Sorry, Mrs Allison,' I sighed, 'but we're not going to lay a hand on little Joey.'

'You're not?' she frowned.

'Nope.'

'We're not?' Janine growled.

'Nope.'

'You *aren't*?' Joey sat up in bed and grinned.

'Nope.'

'Please?' said Mrs Allison.

'Please,' begged Janine.

'Uh-uh.'

'I thought not,' Joey stood. 'You wouldn't dare, would you? You guys think you're really tough, but you wouldn't like to take on Joey Allison, would you? I can do what I like, 'cos I can buy all of you a million times over.' He giggled repulsively.

'Mrs Allison?' siad Janine softly. 'How much for a sock on the jaw?'

'Depends how hard.'

'Not very. Just enough to break it a leetle, leetle bit.'

'Oh, broken jaw,' Mrs Allison mused. 'There's a precedent for that. Allowing for medical fees, loss of earnings, psychological damage, and taking inflation into account . . .' she looked up from her calculator, 'four million, seven hundred and forty-seven dollars and fifty cents. We'll forget the forty-seven fifty if you like.'

Janine's eyes narrowed. 'Can I pay in instalments?'

'Sure, we'll arrange something. Go on. Clout him good and hard.'

'She wouldn't dare!' Joey smirked. He looked up at Janine's forehead. 'Gee, I gave you a beauty, didn't I?'

A strange, deep, entirely animal noise came from somewhere very low down in Janine. 'Whoah, girl,' I breathed. I held her back.

'No,' I said casually. 'You see, we aren't spoiled, talentless little brats. We don't fire sling-shots at innocent people. We don't get any pleasure from hurting others. We could of course sue *you* for the injuries that you have caused. What do you reckon, Mrs Allison? Is this lot worth a hundred thousand?'

'Possibly,' she admitted.

'But we won't even do that, because, you see, we're decent guys. You've hurt us, but do we want revenge?' I looked round at Winston and Ray. They grinned and nodded. 'No!' I said. 'We do

71

not. And why? Because we're not mean, low-down loathsome little psychopaths. We will leave now, with the dignity befitting upstanding American gentlemen. I bid you good day, Mrs Allison.' I turned and made for the door.

'What a load of bull!' cried Joey with glee.

'You mean you aren't going to do *anything* to him?' Mrs Allison plucked at my sleeve.

'Nope.'

'*Please*,' she begged. 'Just beat him up a bit! I'll give you a discount.'

'Sorry.' I pushed open the door and led the others out into the sunshine.

'You can kill him for just twenty million, honest!' she pleaded behind me. 'Easy terms! Low interest!'

I ignored her.

'Peter, what the hell happened to you in there?' Janine demanded. 'All that holier-than-thou, forgiveness and universal love stuff.'

'My dear Janine,' I said, deeply hurt, 'I am universally known for my nobility of spirit, my forbearance and my good will to my fellow man. People stop me in the street and point me out. "There," they say, "is the natural successor to Sir Galahad. His strength," they cry, "is as the strength of ten men, because his heart is pure!" Have you not read of the movement to have the Nobel Peace Prize awarded to me annually?'

'No,' said Janine. 'What's your game, Peter?'

'No game. I am dedicated to non-violence.

72

Now, if you will excuse me, I must have a word with my friends the Mactavishes.'

They gawped at me as I trudged back towards the castle. They could not see the broad grin of gleeful anticipation on my face as I pushed open the main door. 'Angus!' I called, 'Murray! Iain! I've got work for you!'

Chapter Twelve

'Now,' said Finkelstein, 'you are going to be a brafe little boy, not so? Ve are going to haff no tantrums, no unprofessional veeping and moaning today, ja?'

'Yeth, Mithter Finkelthtein,' Joey lisped, and his eyebrows fluttered. He would die young, his expression seemed to say. Heaven had lent him to corrupt mankind for a short while only, and then he would be gathered up again like a little flower, once more to adorn Paradise. No guilt could touch those sweet features, nor age cloud the clarity of those innocent eyes. His little body would be laid to rest and beautiful blossoms would spring up all around. People would come from miles around to reflect in gratitude upon so brief and pure a life, and they would go away enriched and give up drink and take up charity work instead.

It really made me feel quite sick just to think about it.

'So vot happens today, sanks to our splentit special effects persons, is zat Joey is snatched by ze ghosts of ze castle and is in mortal dancher ven Clyde returns, viz his broadsvord he fights ze ghosts und rescues Joey. Is understood? Good.'

'Excuse me, Mr von Finkelstein,' Craig Clyde

swaggered forward. 'There's just one thing about not knowing what's gonna happen. Can these special effects guys make sure that it's my left profile in shot all the time? There's a slight blemish beneath my eye on the right hand side . . .'

'Oh, yeah?' said Janine. 'Let's have a look.' She leaned forward. 'Nothing there,' she shrugged, 'just the usual wrinkles.'

Craig Clyde's mouth fell open. His fists clenched. He shuddered from head to foot in deep revulsion. '*Who* is this woman?' he demanded in ringing tones.

'She's with us, Mr Clyde,' said Winston.

'And she's short-sighted, right?' he forced vitamin pills into his mouth with a trembling hand.

'Oh, yes. Of course. Terrible problems you have, don't you, Janine? Almost blind in fact, aren't you, Janine?'

'Oh, yeah,' Janine snapped.

'I am very sorry to hear it,' Craig Clyde spoke stiffly. 'Having A1 vision myself, I am deeply sympathetic. You see, dear, that is not,' he shuddered again, 'a wrinkle. One does not get wrinkles at twenty-nine. It is an unsightly blemish caused by a nervous condition.'

'Oh,' muttered Janine. 'Yeah, I got the same complaint, and I'm only thirteen.' She sat and folded her arms. 'Jerk,' she said under her breath.

The Mactavishes were obviously feeling a little better by the time filming started. Joey, it had been decided, was lying in bed when strange things started stirring. Again doors creaked, the candle flame flickered and went out. Joey shivered and tried to sleep again, then the curtain blew in on a great wind, the window banged open, the bedclothes were pulled slowly off and Joey was lifted from the bed and borne away.

Murray, who plainly had the makings of a director, orchestrated all this very smoothly. Angus picked up Joey and carried him very gently out of the room. The camera tracked the floating child down the stairs. Angus opened a door and he and Joey passed through. Cut.

The next scene was set in the castle dungeons and here, Finkelstein ordered, Joey was to be tormented by the spirits which haunted *Dunmoanin*. The ghosts rattled chains and groaned a bit. Joey looked suitably terrified. Then the three brothers Mactavish started to enjoy themselves.

First they played catch with Joey, picking him up and flinging him about the room as easily as if he were a football. Joey yelped quite a lot as he was tossed from one pair of invisible hands to another. Occasionally they failed to catch him and then he yelped a whole lot more.

We were then privileged to see a great piece of acting. Suspended in mid-air and lying on his front, Joey kicked and screamed almost as though an invisible hand was descending upon his backside. Again and again he executed this brilliant little mime. His face went very red and somehow, even without glycerine or onions, he managed to produce real tears. It was a treat to behold. When at last he dropped, groaning and drooling to the floor, and Finkelstein ordered 'Cut!' I was the first to get up and applaud.

'Stupendous!' shouted Finkelstein. 'Vonderful. For zis you get ze Oscar. Is brilliant stuff!'

'Is indeed,' agreed the ghostbusters.

Joey wiped the tears from his eyes and stood shakily. He accepted Finkelstein's compliments with a weak sort of smile, but when he looked over at us, there was murder – and understanding – in his eyes. He did not look like an angel any more. He might even live to a ripe old age.

It couldn't last. For a week, the Mactavishes reluctantly did their business, but they were list-less, moody and depressed. Even the prospect of the evening's feasting seemed to have lost its charm. Again and again they disobeyed orders or stomped off set in protest, and they were becom-ing careless in their work. I can't stand a sloppy spook.

Things came to a head on the day when we discovered what Craig Clyde wore beneath his kilt.

With a lack of concern for authenticity, Craig had been turning up day after day in different tartans. 'Isn't it gorgeous,' he'd say of a lurid red and yellow plaid. 'I just saw it and thought "this is me". I just had to have it. It brings out my rich golden tan, don't you think?' or 'I decided on this blue today. So fetching, and a perfect match for my steely blue eyes.' At which Janine, now disillusioned for life about films and film stars, would say something like 'yuk'.

On that Tuesday morning, we were setting up a big scene in the great hall, and all the Mactavishes were standing watching from the gallery when Craig swaggered in in a kilt of red and green. I recognized it at once and my heart sank.

The Macdonald tartan.

'No! Hold on!' I shouted, as the Mactavishes growled and started to move forward, the three brothers at their head.

All the actors and cameramen looked at me as though I were mad. The Mactavishes kept on coming. The brothers were now at the foot of the stairs. 'Stay back!' I said, then, to Craig, 'I really think you should change that kilt, Mr Clyde. Our, um, special effects today won't work with red.'

'What are you talking about?' he sneered. He casually threw another sixteen vitamin pills down his gullet. 'It's a delicious tartan. I had it specially made up.'

'Yes,' I said nervously, one eye on the advancing clansmen, 'but – oh, God – Egon, have you got the, um, special effects guns?'

'Nope,' he shrugged, 'we left 'em in Ecto 1.'

'Oh, hell,' I sighed. 'Come on, guys. We'd better line up and get beaten up.'

'Vot is happening?' asked Finkelstein amiably.

'Our, er, special effects are a little out of

control,' I explained as I flew through the air, projected by one sweep of Angus's giant forearm. The wall hit my shoulder very hard. A moment later, Winston landed in my lap, forcing most of the wind out of me.

What with pushing Winston out of the way, shaking my head and rubbing my shoulder it was some time before I could see what was going on.

What was going on was not good news.

Craig Clyde's distinguished if diminutive frame hung by one foot from Angus's great hairy hand. Angus swung him a little, like a commuter with a briefcase. He looked grim. Craig was screaming something muffled about blood pressure and his analyst. His face was hidden by his kilt, but a large number of other bits of him were exposed. Scotsmen, it is said, wear nothing beneath the kilt. Craig Clyde, I am glad to say, wore something. To be more exact, he wore long thick woollen bloomers with teddy-bears printed on them.

Angus carried Craig slowly up the stairs. 'Put me down!' Craig was hollering. 'This is an outrage! A trauma like this can add years to my age. Help! Help!'

'We'd better go after them,' Winston breathed.

'Oh, dear,' I sighed, 'I suppose so.'

We pulled ourselves to our feet and ran across to the foot of the stairs. Unfortunately, Angus and his brothers were now followed by their troops, so the transfixed camera crews were treated to the spectacle of the Ghostbusters climbing the stairs only to be hurled this way and that by invisible forces whilst, all the while, Craig, teddy-bear-printed bloomers and all, floated upside down above our heads.

Angus, Murray and Iain passed through a door and, still followed by their clan, up another, narrower flight of stairs. We followed, keeping our distance. Craig's cries spiralled down to us in the circular walls. We were bound for the top of the castle's highest tower. This worried me. I did not think that Craig would like plummeting very much. It would almost certainly add years to his age.

We missed that bit, though I have since seen it on film (Finkelstein had the presence of mind to rush outside with a hand-held camera). The film shows the upside-down Craig emerging above the castle's battlements. He wriggles with especial vigour as he is held out beyond the castle walls, about a hundred feet above the ground. His face, though only vaguely visible at that distance, looks like one large screaming mouth as the wind blows the kilt away.

Then, I suppose, Angus just let him go. With a long shrill wail of terror, Craig Clyde plunged downward. His arms flapped twice before he reached ground level.

It was good luck, not good aim on Angus's part, that caused Craig to land in the moat. It was good luck too that he was so stiff with terror that he plunged in head first. The film shows him emerging a long time afterwards, spluttering and coughing and floundering and totally bald save for a few straggling strands of weed.

The film is now a collector's item and commands enormous prices. Craig Clyde has given up movie-making and keeps bees somewhere in the Catskills.

Chapter Thirteen

Shooting was cancelled for the rest of the day, and, as soon as we had collected our proton-guns from Ecto 1, we took the opportunity to have it out with the Mactavishes.

'It won't do, Angus,' Winston said sternly. 'We told you. No-one must get hurt. You could have killed that guy!'

'We should have done,' Angus grunted. 'Did he no' wear the plaid o' the Macdonalds? Nae man has crossed the threshold of Dunmoanin dressed in that vile garb and lived tae to tell the tale. Anyhow, he's a silly wee man.'

'That's as may be,' Winston said patiently, 'but you cannot kill people because they're silly.'

'Why no'?' Murray frowned.

We all searched for an answer to that one, but couldn't think of one. 'You just can't,' was the best that Winston could manage.

'I'm fed up wi' the whole business,' said Iain.

'Aye, me too,' Angus scowled.

'But we've got a deal,' I objected.

'We don't care for your deal any more.'

'You know what that means?' I warned.

'Aye, ye'll be wanting a wee fight.'

'I'm afraid so. We can't just have you wandering

around making nuisances of yourselves and chopping people's heads off, you know. It's illegal and Unamerican and not very nice.'

'Aye, well, we all have to have our little hobbies.'

'So we fight,' I shrugged. 'Mr Finkelstein won't like it.'

'Och, that little tub of a man doesna matter,' Iain spat. 'Anyhow, since ye disposed o' the Macdonalds, life has seemed purposeless.'

'Aye,' Angus nodded. 'Daft, is it no'? For centuries we hate them, then as soon as they're gone, we miss 'em.'

'Nothing to do all day,' Murray wiped a tear from his eye. 'It's terrible boring.'

'Over a week wi'out a decapitation,' Iain sighed. 'It's no' natural. The men are out of condition.'

'Ghosts will be ghosts,' said Ray.

'And Mactavishes will be Mactavishes,' Angus nodded.

'Right, then,' Egon stood, all business like. 'We meet tonight, for the last time.'

'Ye'll no' find it as easy as you think,' Murray bragged. 'We have, shall we say, a few little surprises amongst the domestic pets.'

'Is that right?' I smiled. 'Well, I'm sure we can manage. We are The Real Ghostbusters. Not much frightens us.'

'We shall see, my brave wee manikin,' Angus's beard spread in a grin. 'We shall see!'

* * *

'What do you think he meant about pets, Peter?' asked Ray as we checked and cleaned our weapons in the hotel that night.

'I dunno,' I shrugged. 'Can't be anything too bad. We've seen most things.'

'I suppose so.'

'I mean, we know they've got dogs. They look pretty mean, but they ran away last time.'

'Yeah.'

'You've got no records of anything worse. Have you?'

'Uh-uh. No animals.'

'It's probably all bluff.' I sauntered over to the window and gazed out on the lights of the town below. In the corner behind an armchair, Slimer, who had a stomach ache, groaned deeply.

'You realize that this will mean the end of our work here?' I said.

'Yup,' said Winston, 'back to good old New York. I can't wait.'

'Shouldn't think Fink'll pay us for the remaining weeks.'

'Ah, well,' Winston peered down the muzzle of his ghost-trap, 'money isn't everything.'

I looked closely at the shape of his head. I'm sure there must be something physical which makes people says things like that.

'I was rather thinking,' said Egon quietly, 'that I might stay out here.'

'*What*?' We all turned on him.

'What are you talking about, Egon?' I

demanded, only it came out more like a husky squeak than a demand.

'Well,' Egon bleated, 'the fact of the matter is that I have of late developed amatorious feelings in relation to Louella Rossini,' he blushed, 'and she has been gracious enough to indicate that she reciprocates these sentiments . . .'

'You mean you've fallen for her,' snapped Janine. 'Pathetic.'

'It's something in the water. It must be. Egon,' I laid a hand on his shoulder, 'you are usually an intelligent, level-headed sort of guy. Now, please, let us study the facts. Here we have exhibit A, Egon Spengler, a bespectacled, penniless ghost-buster. And here is exhibit B, a multi-millionairess siren of the silver screen who marries and divorces like other people change shoes. Is there a connection between these two creatures? Are they Barrett and Browning, Laurel and Hardy, cup and saucer, Astaire and Rogers? There is not. They are as alike as, say, Alexander the Great and Mahatma Gandhi, Shirley Temple and Errol Flynn . . .'

'Boy George and Ernest Hemingway,' supplied Janine.

'Orlando and Rin-tin-tin,' said Ray.

'Chalk and Cheese,' said Winston. I studied his head again. There must *be* a reason.

'You do not understand,' Egon looked aggrieved. 'Amor,' he said, 'vincit omnia.'

'It's no good quoting diseases at us,' I told him.

'No,' he explained, 'it means "love conquers all".'

'Yes, but, to quote the good book, "money answereth everything," and you ain't got none. Listen, old egghead, Louella Rossini thinks that you are the greatest special effects man she's ever seen. She reckons you can make fortunes and will soon dominate the movie business. Fact is, you don't know a special effect from a terrapin. It's the ghosts which have been doing the tricks on this movie, Egon, not you.'

'Such mercenary considerations do not concern Miss Rossini,' said Egon pompously. 'She also believes that I have potential as an actor, a fact of which I have always been aware.'

'You, an actor?'

'Yes, actually. I have experience in the theatre.'

'Oh, yeah? Where was that?'

'At high school. I was a good actor.'

'What was your biggest role?'

'Thrdngl,' he stated proudly.

'What?'

'Third angel.'

'In the nativity play?'

'Yes. But I got a good review.'

'Don't tell me, "Charming performances were also given by . . ."'

'There you are,' Egon nodded self-righteously, 'even you read it.'

There was silence for a moment while we all studied our poor old friend. He looked around at each of us in turn. He seemed to be squinting down his nose.

'Egon,' I said at last, 'what are you doing with your face?'

'I am gazing at you from under heavy-lidded eyes,' he drawled, 'in an Elegant but Masterful Manner. Louella says it's rather good.'

'Louella,' said Ray, 'would tell you that she likes your fungus collection. She's using you, for God's sake! She thinks you're the world's greatest magician.'

'Be careful, please, Ray,' Egon stopped squinting and forced out his lower jaw. He looked very much like a monkey. 'You are speaking of the woman of whom I am enamoured. Besides, she does like fungus. I gave her a specimen of *Mycorhodocarpus rubens* and she said it was, and I quote, "the cutest little mould" she'd ever been given. So there.'

'This,' I said sadly, 'is a problem to be dealt with later. For the moment, the Ghostbusters must go back to what they do best. Everyone ready?'

'Ready.' Ray and Winston stood and rattled their guns.

'Egon?'

'What?' he looked blearily up at me, 'Oh,' he blinked, 'yes, I suppose so.' He too stood.

'Right,' I said, 'be seeing you, Janine.'

'Don't rush back on my account,' she yawned, and from Slimer's corner came a deep, mournful groan of farewell.

Chapter Fourteen

There was no moon this time. The sky was pitch black as we approached the castle. We trod as softly as we could manage with all the kit that we were carrying, but the Mactavishes heard us coming.

I will never know how Winston was aware of the rock hurtling down at us from the tower. He could not have seen it in the total blackness, but something made him gasp, 'Look out!' and we stepped back just as a large chunk of battlement crashed into the drawbridge a few feet ahead of us.

'So much for the element of surprise,' I muttered. 'Watch the portcullis. One – two – three – go!' Together we flung ourselves into the doorway. Even before I hit the ground, I heard the grinding of metal above us. A second later, the great black spikes of the portcullis slammed down on to the stone with a clang.

'They mean business,' Winston panted.

'Yup. This could take longer than we thought. They'll be waiting for us in the great hall. Someone's got to go in there and turn on the lights.'

'You got it,' Winston pulled himself to his feet. 'Give me covering fire.'

We nodded and stood with our backs to the great door. Again I counted, 'One, two, three and – hit it!' Egon flung the door open and Winston, crouching and weaving, vanished into the darkness. We fired over his head, bombarding the gallery with ions. Masonry crashed. Somewhere someone grunted. Scottish voices gabbled urgently. Suddenly the great hall was flooded with light. We swung round the doorframe to join Winston, guns blazing.

A kilt vanished through a doorway on the gallery. Only four ghosts were trapped in the corner of the great hall nearest the door. Egon and Winston finished them off easily enough.

'We've got to go after them,' Egon panted, 'and it's gonna be nasty. They could be lying in wait anywhere in this pile.'

'No choice, though,' Ray breathed. 'They're not gonna come back here with all these lights.'

'Better split up into pairs,' I whispered. I turned to Winston and Ray. 'You guys take the left. We'll take the right.'

Ray nodded and saluted. Together we climbed up to the gallery and split up.

So much of our work is done in the dark that Egon has developed a pretty efficient sort of miner's helmet with a light at the front. We were grateful for them now. Not only did they give some light, they also gave me at least a little extra confidence with regard to falling masonry and glancing claymores.

With our 'sniffers' in our left hands, our proton-guns in our right, we walked the long dark echoing corridors. At each door, we stopped. One of us would fling open the door and charge in, firing, while the other held the doorway. On the ground floor, we found nothing but two shaggy ghost dogs and, rather suprisingly, a ghost mouse in the kitchen. We captured them, then came to the stairwell.

The first attack came there. We were halfway up when the barrage of stones began. They were about the size of the average brick, but they were hurled with force and they hurt. There was hysterical laughter above as we retreated to the safety of the corridor. 'Is there any other way up there?' I whispered.

Egon considered for a moment, then nodded. 'Has to be,' he said. 'The kitchen's beneath the main dining-hall. There has to be some kind of dumb-waiter.'

'Good thinking,' I sighed, thinking how much the Ghostbusters would miss Egon. 'Let's get back there.'

We scurried on tiptoe to the empty kitchen. Only the hooks in the ceiling and the huge old cooking range now remained of what must once have been a scene of warmth and bustle. At the far end, however, on the other side of a door from the stove, there was a wooden cabinet. We cautiously applied the 'sniffer' to its door. No reading. I opened it.

The dumb-waiter was a cramped, cobwebby wooden box about the size of a tea-chest. It looked as if it had not been used for centuries. I tentatively tugged at the age-blackened ropes. 'I hope to God these things hold,' I whispered fervently.

'OK,' I turned to Egon, 'you pull me up as quietly as you can. Then you run back to the stairs and set up that trap. I'll give you a count of five before I start blasting, OK?'

'OK,' Egon nodded. 'Good luck, Peter,' he smiled.

'And you.'

I clambered into the little box. It rocked, but held my weight, for the time being at least. It had been designed for food, and would have provided plenty of room for a leg of lamb or a boar's head. I had to sit completely doubled up, my knees clasped close to my chest. If anyone was up there waiting for me, I would be in no position to defend myself.

I nodded to Egon. He reached forward and, very slowly, wincing at each creak, pulled on the rope.

I started slowly to rise. I reached up and switched off the lamp on my helmet. I'd have to do this in the dark. First I could see Egon's face as he tugged. Sweat made a quicksilver sheen on his brow. Then the strip of light beneath me narrowed until I could see nothing but his feet, hear nothing but his breathing. Then there was darkness, and silence save for the creaking of the wood, the slight grinding of the pulley with each upward movement.

I did not know what to expect when I reached the dining-hall. I did know, however, that, for a few seconds at least, my head would be visible yet I would be incapable of moving. The thought was not a pleasing one.

The experience was decidedly worse. If Egon had been trying to torment me, he could not have done a better job. On the first tug, my forehead alone emerged in the little band of light. On the second, my head and the upper part of my chest were exposed. Then Egon paused for breath.

I could see the ghosts gathered about the fire-place in the flickering light of the flames. There were perhaps thirty of them. Iain the Bullslayer stood at their centre. They were drinking and laughing. Some of them held drawn swords. If one of them turned my way, I'd be going back to the kitchen carved into convenient sized oven-ready portions.

'Och,' said Iain, 'how many men can claim that they've stayed alive and fightin' for three hundred and fifty years? I've no taste for this new-fangled life in America, and I'll go happy enough into the laddies' little boxy, but I'd like to tak a few on' em wi' me.'

'Aye!' the men raised their glasses, and Egon, as if on cue, pulled. I was clear, but still had to get out and free my weapons. I did not look forward to that.

First, trusting to the darkness and the crackling of the fire, I carefully slid my legs out of the box, then, very slowly and very carefully, I eased the gun round my back and laid it across my lap. At least now, if they turned and saw me, I could defend myself, but I had to think of attack as well. If I drove them from this room – and it seemed unlikely that I could do so without receiving a dagger in the chest – they might turn left on the corridor rather than right towards the staircase. I could only pray that Egon could draw their attention and their fire so that I could drive them down into his trap.

I prayed.

Egon's shout came first, then a cry from one of the men on watch on the landing. Iain laughed and threw his glass into the fireplace. The others copied him and followed him to the door. Amidst the crashing and hissing, they did not hear me as I slid from the dumb-waiter and stood.

I followed them out on to the landing. They leaned over the balcony, jeering and flinging rocks from a pile beneath the railing.

'Where's your wee friend, then?' roared Iain, 'he's all gob and nae fight!'

'Right behind you, Iain,' I said, and I pulled the trigger. They turned as the first salvo hit them. They looked around desperately, realizing that there could be no escape. Some of them raised their swords and made to rush towards me but I calmly kept up the fusillade. Suddenly something flashed in Iain's hand. I ducked, and a small, wicked blade span past my left ear and clattered on the bare boards behind me.

I took a step forward. They were yielding before the pressure of my fire. Already some of them, screaming curses, retreated down the stairs. Egon moved backward into the doorway. Blood streamed from a cut just above his hairline. There was a livid red gash on his jaw.

'Go on,' I murmured, and I kept my finger tightly curled about the trigger. 'Go on, you crazed ghouls. Give up. You haven't got a hope . . .'

The first of the ghosts was now nearing Egon's trap. He shrieked as he reverted once more to ectoplasmic vapour and was sucked in, but it was a wild, jubilant shriek, I think, not one of pain. The Mactavishes knew that this was the end. Now they could battle forever with their beloved enemies in our containment unit back in New York.

Every one of them fought and cursed to the last. Every one of them was forced back into the trap. Last of all went Iain the Bullslayer, who gave a great cry of 'Mactavish!' and swung his mighty sword twice above his head. The cry was still echoing in the walls as Egon leaned forward to switch off the trap.

'Phew!' I breathed. 'You OK, Egon?'

'Yeah,' he said dully. 'Few cuts and bruises, but otherwise all right.'

I trudged wearily down the stairs. 'How many'd we get?'

'I counted twenty-six.'

'Half their force. S'pose we'd better go and give the others a hand.'

We picked up the ghost-trap and returned to the great hall. Everything was disturbingly still, and our footsteps rang down the corridor ahead of us.

Chapter Fifteen

Ray and Winston were waiting for us. They too looked tired. They too bore the scars of battle. 'Hi, guys,' I greeted them. 'Get 'em?'

'Yup.' Winston wiped his brow.

'How many?'

'Twenty-five, including Murray. Never seen a spook stand up to so much proton fire, and at the end, he drained a glass of whisky, yelled "Mactavish!" and went laughing to his doom.'

'That leaves Angus,' Egon said glumly.

'And not only Angus,' said a deep voice behind us. We span around. Angus stood on the gallery. He leaned forward, his fists clasping the railing. He wore a tam o'shanter, a kilt and a sash in the Mactavish tartan. The sash was clasped at the shoulder with a giant emerald brooch. His tunic was of black velvet with bright silver buttons. A vast foaming ruffle of lace swelled his chest. A bejewelled sword hung at his right side and, at his left, a great horn mounted in gold.

When we had recovered from the first effects of this magnificent apparition, we darted forward to do battle, but he raised his right hand. 'Nay, nay,' he purred, 'ye can wait a minute mair. I'll come to your canny wee trap soon enough, and welcome.

But first, there is one thing tha' I must do, as the last laird of Dunmoanin and the Isles of Addle-daig. It is a secret passed on to me by my father on his deathbed as by every laird to his son throughout history.'

He stood up straight and raised the great horn to his lips.

'Stop him!' cried Egon, but already the blast of the horn filled the castle.

I have often tried to describe that sound. It was deep as a bull's call, yet high and silvery as a cornet. It was loud enough to shake the whole building yet somehow it seemed to throb softly, even melodiously in the night air. Egon and Winston were wasting no time in listening. Angus was evaporating but the sound of the horn grew no weaker. Even when he had completely vanished into the ghost-trap, the blast still seemed to mount, reaching far, far across the continents and the centuries.

At last it died, though it rang in my head for minutes afterward.

'Well,' said Ray, 'that's the lot of 'em.'

'I don't think so,' I said grimly.

'What?'

'That horn. He was calling something or some-one. Listen.'

Everyone fell silent. At first the noise from outside sounded merely like some distant stranger walking on gravel, but it came nearer and nearer, louder and louder, and now it sounded like an

97

army on the march. Whatever it was, it should not have been in Hollywood after midnight.

I rushed to the great door and pulled it open. 'Ray!' I called, 'the portcullis!'

I tried to focus on whatever it was that was moving out there. It was too large to be identifiable, but it was alive. I could hear its breathing, see the movement of its flesh.

The portcullis grated as it rose. 'Come on!' I yelled. The others ran out after me. We stopped. We looked. 'Dear God,' I was suddenly very short of breath.

'Sheesh!' breathed Winston at my right ear.

'But how come we've no record of this?' asked Ray.

'It's natural habitat would have been the loch beneath *Dunmoanin*,' Egon said calmly. 'As a ghost, it could have stayed beneath the waters for centuries without anyone seeing it.'

For the shape and the size of the mysterious creature lumbering up the slope were now clearly discernible against the soft glow of the sky above Los Angeles. At the shoulder, it was roughly the height of the castle. It had a small head and a body as long as the average church nave. Its tail swished slowly, sweeping the shacks and caravans of the film set away like toys.

'Extraordinary,' said Egon, 'it closely resembles the diplodoccus, though the weight and the length of the forelegs recalls the Brachiosaurus. The armoured plates on the spinal column, on the

98

other hand, are more usually associated with, say, the Stegosaurus. Nothing like it has ever been seen before. I shall call it . . .'

'Egon,' I reminded him, 'it is coming nearer, and it looks hostile. It's name can wait. What the hell are we going to do about it?'

'I can't see the proton guns having much effect,' he said calmly. 'We'll just have to hope that it's carnivorous. Highly unlikely, of course, but if it is, it can be lured into a trap.'

'How?' I asked stupidly.

'Well, one of us will have to be the bait. The others will have to operate the traps.'

'I'll be the bait,' I said. I cannot think why. It must have been a slip of the tongue. The others did not seem to object. They just drew aside and let me face the oncoming monster.

There are lots of unpleasant things about standing in the path of an overgrown newt. One which I hadn't considered was the smell. This creature, whose beady eyes I could now see clearly, had a serious personal hygiene problem. Get a load of wet leaves, a lot of old fish, mix with stagnant water and leave for three hundred and fifty years to mature. Dab lightly behind the ears and you'll be a wow in the discos and dance-halls frequented by prehistoric Scottish monsters.

It was about ten yards from me now. The smell and the heat of its breath was overpowering. It still seemed not to have noticed me, and it had to be stopped, so I took aim at its left eye and let it have a blast. It squealed and stopped. It raised a foreleg to scratch its injured eye, then lowered its head and searched for its assailant. Its eyesight was obviously poor, for its head, about whose smallness I was beginning to change my mind, was little more than five yards away, yet still it seemed not to see me.

'Are you ready?' I shouted at the Ghostbusters.

'Not quite!' called Egon from somewhere near the beast's hind legs. 'We've got to link up all three traps! We need an overflow system, otherwise the traps'll blow and we'll have all the Mactavishes and this creature on the loose!'

'Well, hurry up, will you?' I cried. The monster had raised its head again and now lifted a foot to take a further step forward. I had to keep it where it was. I gave it another blast.

This time, it roared with pain and irritation and scratched furiously at its eye. Its search was quicker and more eager now. It snuffled at the ground like a spaniel.

'Nearly ready!' shouted Winston. I saw Ray scampering beneath the creature's hind legs, an extension ecto-cable in his hand.

I shot the beast again, this time on the nose. It saw me then. I got to see its tonsils.

It opened its mouth wide in a savage snarl. It had a large number of teeth, all of which looked very sharp. The smell was overpowering. I reeled, suddenly faint, and prayed that it was the sort of beast which had table manners and picked up its food rather than eating it off the floor.

'Come on!' I shouted to Egon. Now I was firing continually down the beast's throat. If I ran backward, the monster would have to move forward in pursuit and all the work with the traps would have to start again. I sidestepped, therefore, as a huge clawed paw struck at me, and scurried between its forelegs. I fired upward at its chest. It backed up, now really angry. 'Come on, Egon! I can't hold it much longer!'

'OK!' Egon rapped, 'we're ready! Just let Winston get out of . . . yaaagh!' he screamed as the beast's tail sent him flying.

'Go for it, Ray!' I shrieked as the huge claw ripped my boiler suit. I felt blood trickling cold down my back, then the slimy soft pads of the monster's paws closed about me and squeezed tight, and my feet left the ground.

'Go for it!' I shrieked, as I rose nearer to the monster's stinking mouth. '*Now!*'

And suddenly the grip on my body slackened. A little whimper shuddered through the beast and I was dropping fast. I landed heavily and pitched forward. I rolled. Above me, the monster grunted, straining to escape, then started to fade and break up like an image in an old photograph.

The monster of Dunmoanin was history.

We had serious problems getting home. Not only were we all aching, bruised and bleeding, but, what with the complete clan Mactavish and their pet, there was altogether too much anti-matter in the ghost-traps.

The aviation boys should look into spectre-power. Egon would have floated up into the stratosphere had we not clung to his feet as we made our way back to Ecto 1.

We were all exhausted, but none of us, I think, slept too well that night.

Chapter Sixteen

'So, my excellent special effects persons,' Finkelstein greeted us the following morning, 'but – you are all bruised and cut! Vot is ze matter?'

'We, um, had a little accident with the car,' I replied. 'Listen, Mr Finkelstein, we need a word with you. In private.'

He glanced quickly at me, then nodded. 'All right,' he murmured, then, to the crew, 'OK, take fife! I must consult viz zese chentlemen.'

He led us away to a spot behind the caterers' caravan. 'Vot – er, I mean – what the hell's been going on here, guys? Caravans smashed to smithereens, shacks knocked down, serious damage to the interior of the castle, huge fake footprints everywhere? It's crazy.'

'Yeah, well, we had a bit of trouble. That's what we wanted to talk to you about. You've got no more special effects, Jack.'

'You – you destroyed my ghosts?' Finkelstein turned very red. 'You – you – but you can't!' he squeaked.

'Sorry, Jack,' Winston shrugged, 'they gave us no choice.'

'They got a little – out of hand,' I explained. 'It was them or us. You saw what they did yesterday.'

'I can afford actors!' Finkelstein protested. 'I cannot afford effects like what them spooks were supplying! I would have made my fortune,' he span round and round, gazing at his pudgy hands, working himself into a frenzy. 'Millions and millions!' he blubbered. 'Academy awards! And you! You! Four nobodies from New York, you destroy my ghosts without permission! There must be a law about it! I'll sue you. You can't just go round destroying other people's ghosts.'

'Sorry, Jack,' I told him, 'but ghosts are common property, a common enemy of all mankind. Look at it this way. You didn't expect the spooks when you came here. You just expected to make a movie, right? So you got a few days' free special effects. That's a bonus. Say thank you and make the most of it. Easy come, easy go, right?'

'No!' Finkelstein sobbed and stamped like a spoiled child. 'It was not for that that I employed you. Your job was to look after them, soothe them, make them feel good, keep them working! I coulda made them into stars! They coulda worked on a hundred films. I had it all planned. Musicals with girls dancing with invisible partners, *The Dear Haunter, The Sound of Mucus, Bogy Boogie Woogie* . . .'

'Yeah, yeah,' Winston broke in, 'but we told you from the beginnin'. We're Ghostbusters. That's our job. And you just can't trust a ghost. There's nothing more we could have done. Sorry.'

'Well,' Finkelstein sniffed and wiped his nose.

'What's done is done. As long as you don't expect to get paid.'

'Oh no, why should we?' Winston sang in an ironic falsetto. 'I mean we've just been shot at by a psychopathic midget, nearly killed by a collection of crazed Caledonian ghouls and half torn apart by a resentful diplodocus . . .'

'A little more like the Brachiosaurus,' put in Egon.

'You mean you *destroyed* a monster?' Finkelstein squeaked. 'Never have I heard of such unprofessional behaviour. Why didn't you keep it and wait till we had the cameras rolling?'

'We didn't have a hutch of the right size handy, Jack,' I sighed. 'Look, we've given you a ton of footage unparalleled in cinema history. We deserve something for that.'

'Sure, sure,' Finkelstein patted the air, 'you've earned your expenses . . .'

'Our *expenses*?' we cried, outraged.

'You think that's nothing? I'd've paid you for your week's work, guys, honest I would, but the food bill at that hotel! I mean, OK, ghostbusting may take it out of a man, but this is ridiculous!'

'Thanks, Slimer,' I groaned.

'Not at all,' said Jack Fink.

'So what I'm going to do is this,' Egon nodded keenly and blinked, 'I'm going to give her this rare *conferva pulverulens aquatica* which grew on the spleen of a sperm whale . . .'

'She'll swoon with delight,' I assured him.

'. . . and I'll say, "Louella, of late I have experienced, as doubtless you are aware, sensations not to mince words, of an amatory nature, in relation to your person."'

'She'll melt.'

'"Alas," I shall say, "I am not what I appear. I have been engaged in a necessary dissimulation. You thought me a cinematographic prestidigitator . . ."'

'Seductive stuff. Does that mean special effects man?'

'In essence, yes. "But," I shall continue, "I have hitherto been a quester of ectoplasmic emanations, otherwise known as a Ghostbuster. Those," I shall say sternly, "were not mechanical tricks. You were in fact being picked up and manipulated, as were the objects around you, by the undead."'

'She'll fall into your arms with joy and admiration.'

'"If, therefore," I shall say, and here I believe that it is customary to perform a genuflection . . .'

'Fall on one knee,' I explained to Ray.

'"If therefore, you will consent to enter with me into matrimonial conjugation, I should be deeply honoured and I should resume what I feel to be my innate vocation, that is, the pursuit of a thespian career."'

'Acting,' I translated. 'Right, kid,' I slapped him on the shoulder, 'go to it.'

Egon smiled and blinked at the ground. 'Yes,' he said. 'Right. Nerve-wracking business, wooing.' And he set off for Louella's caravan.

We tried not to listen. We remained a reasonable distance from the caravan, put our hands in our pockets and whistled, as though waiting for a train to arrive.

Louella obviously liked the first bit. There was nothing but contented cooing from the caravan. Knowing what he intended to say, we knew almost to the second when the trouble would start. Somewhere around 'you were in fact being . . . manipulated . . . by the undead.'

There was a shrill shriek of terror and outrage, then a series of bangs and crashes. The soft, gentle tone of her voice disappeared. A very unpleasant metallic twang had entered it. We tried not to listen, but words such as 'no hoper', 'filthy fungus' and 'ghoul' floated inescapably to our ears, together with many others which I shall not record for fear that they will turn the ink blue and make the page unsightly.

Egon emerged a moment later. We all whistled very loudly and looked in the opposite direction.

'Hi, guys,' he bleated.

'Egon!' we turned round, smiling and saying, 'Well I never! How about that? Here's Egon! Whatever next?' and other casual, natural remarks.

Egon wiped something which looked suspiciously like *conferva pulverulens aquatica* from his glasses. 'Miss Rossini,' he said solemnly, 'is not the woman I took her for. I have been foolish. She had no interest in fungus at all, you know. None at all.'

'Good thing you discovered in time, Egon,' Winston nodded sagely. 'Shall we get back to New York?'

And the Ghostbusters, with one voice, cried, 'Yeah!'

Epilogue

Quote from a review of *The Haunted Castle*:

Joey Allison gives his usual competent perform-ance, though the myth of his eternal youth is beginning to wear a little thin. Louella Rossini vamps, Craig Clyde postures. It is all much as you would expect. The biggest disappointment, how-ever, is the special effects, which, to be honest, are neither special nor effective. In an age which offers a wealth of technological wizardry, Mr von Finkel-stein has reverted to ancient stage hokum – flying swords, bodies and so on – using techniques which were patently obvious even in the 'twenties when first they were seen on screen. They are weary clichés and, like all clichés, have lost their power to frighten or affect the modern viewer . . .

I thought of the mighty Mactavishes and their monster, now safely stored in our containment unit in the basement. I was glad that we had zapped them before they could read their reviews.